"I'm not very good at leaving one-night stands..."

Darcy slipped from between the sheets and stuck out her hand, which Tyler looked at incredulously, so she put it down.

"Technically this was our second," he said with a wry grin.

"True, but if I said two-night stand, it would mean two nights in a row." She wrinkled her nose. "Okay, that sounds ridiculous."

"Two one-night stands doesn't sound like enough." He pulled her back down on the bed.

She sighed. "It was really fun." Accepting his long, lingering kiss, she smiled into his beautiful but somewhat bewildered blue-green eyes and got to her feet.

Then realized she was wearing *his* underwear.

"I...um..." She felt a hot flush travel up her spine at the botched exit, and swept her hand down to indicate his shirt and boxers. "I'll, uh, wash these and get them back to you."

"No problem," he said lazily. "Why not come by *tonight...*?"

Blaze™

Dear Reader,

Remember the romantic comedy line Harlequin Duets? I got my start writing for that series and wrote six of them before switching to Blaze. When my editor suggested last spring that I write a book for the Forbidden Fantasies miniseries, my mind immediately started working. Who would most need her life to resemble a fantasy? How about someone who has been caring for sick loved ones for years and is finally free to explore her own needs? Does that sound like a comedy? No, I didn't think so either.

But somehow it turned out to be one. Darcy and Tyler kept me laughing as the most enjoyable couple I've written about in a long while. And their friends Molly and Bruce are people I wish I knew in my own life. I kept feeling as if I was back writing for Duets—except Darcy and Tyler's racy adventures could only be at home in a Blaze.

I hope wherever you live that spring is springing and your love life is blooming.

Cheers,

Isabel Sharpe

P.S. Visit me at www.IsabelSharpe.com

ISABEL SHARPE
Indulge Me

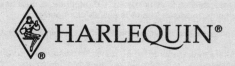

HARLEQUIN®

TORONTO • NEW YORK • LONDON
AMSTERDAM • PARIS • SYDNEY • HAMBURG
STOCKHOLM • ATHENS • TOKYO • MILAN • MADRID
PRAGUE • WARSAW • BUDAPEST • AUCKLAND

ISBN-13: 978-0-373-79397-6
ISBN-10:   0-373-79397-9

INDULGE ME

ABOUT THE AUTHOR

Isabel Sharpe was not born pen in hand like so many of her fellow writers. After she quit work in 1994 to stay home with her first-born son and nearly went out of her mind, she started writing. After more than twenty novels for Harlequin— along with another son—Isabel is more than happy with her choice these days. She loves hearing from readers. Write to her at www.IsabelSharpe.com.

Books by Isabel Sharpe

HARLEQUIN BLAZE

*Men To Do
**Do Not Disturb
†The Wrong Bed
††The Martini Dares
‡It's All About Attitude
‡‡Forbidden Fantasies

Don't miss any of our special offers. Write to us at the following address for information on our newest releases.

Harlequin Reader Service
U.S.: 3010 Walden Ave., P.O. Box 1325, Buffalo, NY 14269
Canadian: P.O. Box 609, Fort Erie, Ont. L2A 5X3

To my patient and wonderful sons,
who tolerated lack of quality mom-time for
far too long so I could finish this book.

1

DARCY WOLF COULDN'T decide whether the view of that one painter hard at work on the ladder scraping the old paint off a second-floor window—the one that was so, um, soooo, well, you know—was better with her sunglasses on or off. So she gave herself permission to experiment thoroughly.

On. Off. On. Off.

Still no decision. But lying here in her backyard on a chaise longue with a cold iced tea made just the way she liked it—strong, no sugar, brewed with mint that sprouted reliably in a bed by the house—feeling the sun, light and warm, not yet the blistering full strength of a Milwaukee summer, with virile young men clambering around her childhood five-bedroom Lannon stone home, well, she'd say life was good. And not to sound selfish, but she deserved a little "good life" after so many years bearing witness to pain and suffering and despair.

Once the painters were done, she would put the house up for sale and, at age twenty-six, finally get her life under way. Four years spent nursing her beloved father to a heartbreaking end when his cancer returned a second time to claim him. Another year after that nursing Greg, her boyfriend of four years, back to health from a head injury he sustained the day she finally broke up with him. A devil inside her still wondered if he'd subconsciously engineered the car accident to punish her or keep her with him, which turned out to be nearly the same thing.

She'd cared for her father devotedly, given him what joy she could, just as he'd given her his life and time and nurturing after her mother died, and she'd grieved over the inevitable slow end that had begun when she was a teenager with his first bout, was put on hold for too few precious years of remission, and had begun again in college. She'd nursed Greg in the other direction—away from death and back to health—with slightly less selflessness. After all that had gone into her agonized decision to leave him…

But she couldn't beat herself up over that anymore. Greg was functioning on his own, nearly back to normal, and a couple of weeks ago she got up her nerve and repeated the ghastly breakup scene, feeling like dirt to cause the poor man even more pain. However, this time she did it at his house in Madison, where she'd lived for the past year while she'd taken care of him, so that she'd be the one driving right after.

And now…

Summer waited around the corner with hot, humid breath and long lazy limbs, but spring had come, and like the new shoots pushing determinedly out of the still-chilly earth, Darcy Wolf was going to bloom. Not here in Wauwatosa, an immediate suburb of Milwaukee, where she'd lived a quarter century plus one year, a city she knew inside out, but off and away, new horizons, new adventures, new life, new Darcy.

She took a sip of the tea, ice cubes rattling appealingly in the bright orange plastic cup she'd bought last summer to brighten her and her father's outdoor living while he could still be up and around. She could afford to buy cups made of gold now if she wanted, though she couldn't imagine why she ever would. Her father's death hadn't been a surprise, but his final gift had been. Money. Money he never so much as hinted he had, from his family and from Mom's family, from a lifetime of success as a wholesale jewelry salesman and from careful living. Her new independence had only just started to sink in. But already she had plans. Who wouldn't? She'd quit her dull job in Madison as office manager for a psychology practice, and as soon as the house was in presentable condition and then sold, she'd take off for distant lands. Or rather, distant states, living as she'd wanted to since she was a girl obsessed with maps and dreaming about travel. Two years in Seattle. Two years in Los Angeles. Two years in Miami. Two years in Boston—the four corners of the country. She'd write about her experiences, volunteer, take ballet lessons, tap-dancing lessons, fencing lessons, learn to paint, to fix cars, to build furniture…

And then? Eventually she wanted to go back to school and build on her education degree with a master's in school counseling. She'd be thirty-four and probably want to settle down somewhere permanently. Maybe she'd even come back here, though secretly she imagined herself becoming so chic and sophisticated that Milwaukee and Wauwatosa would seem like so much beer, cheese and sausage in comparison.

For now, in her backyard with iced tea and a whole life ahead of her tied down to no one, she had another important consideration: her hot painter needed a fantasy name so she wouldn't have to keep referring to him as Her Hot Painter. When she and her friend Molly Johnston were teenagers, poring over a name book to see what they'd choose for their eventual children, they'd discovered—and giggled endlessly over it—that "Garrett" meant "with a mighty spear."

That would do.

The newly christened Garrett scraped back and forth at a spot suffering from too many years of wind, rain, extreme temperatures and not enough extra energy from Darcy to deal with homeowner responsibilities. His biceps showed domed and hard below his sleeve, while triceps ridged the opposite side.

The raised arm pulled up the hem of his white T-shirt and allowed an occasional glimpse of toned abdominal muscle.

The day before, and the day before that, he'd stayed later than the others. She'd spoken to him both times, casual worker-boss conversations. She'd complimented his work, he'd thanked her, they'd talked painting and nothing more. But he'd looked at her as if...

As if, as if, ohhhhh, yes, as if. She loved that *as if.* She could definitely come up with a few delightful fantasy activities involving the two of them.

In the hospitals while her dad or Greg slept, or were otherwise unresponsive, she'd knitted, read, done crossword puzzles—in short, become an expert at passing time. And when she could no longer bear to read or to play word games, well then, sometimes she'd daydream in embarrassingly vivid and erotic detail. Weird, maybe, but give anyone as many hours in a medical facility as she'd had to spend, and he or she would get as sick of grief and pain and frustration—hers and the patient's—and need escape as much as she had. One handsome, brainy doctor and one buff, talented physical therapist had provided, er, stimulation. Her imagination did the rest.

Now that she was out in the real world breathing fresh air instead of *eau de maladie,* no longer trapped by four walls and tough emotions, she could devote even more time—guilt-free—to one of her favorite pastimes. In fact, she could imagine right now that—

Garrett turned his head as if some receptor in his brain had picked up her thoughts.

Darcy didn't even try to pretend she hadn't been facing him, but she was glad for her sunglasses because it was possible he'd think she was asleep. Asleep holding her glass of iced tea. Sure. Why not. Uh-huh.

He nodded and touched the brim of his baseball cap—

Brewers, of course, good Wisconsin man—and then he went back to scraping.

Oh, my my. How busted could she get? But she was single, straight and certainly within her rights to look.

Except now that she'd looked, she kept wanting to look and then look some more, up the strong column of his back to his broad shoulders, imagining them flexing and contracting under the cotton of his T-shirt as he worked. Then back again to his nicely rounded butt and strong legs, which she could imagine in all sorts of quite pleasant positions, as well.

Yum.

Maybe he was the ranch owner and Darcy-Anne, the feisty, abundantly cleavaged city girl who'd just bought the property next door…

Or maybe he'd be the suited sophisticate at the bar, balancing a dry martini, who nearly swallowed his tongue when he saw La Darce strut in, several-times-pierced and poured into black leather…

Or maybe the funky, long-haired student at the art museum who came upon her in a quiet out-of-the-way place, pleasuring herself, and kindly stopped to help…

Garrett turned again, this time tipping his sunglasses down and shooting her a look over them.

Busted again. But she didn't turn away this time, either. She tipped her own sunglasses down and shot him a look over, too. Because why not? Who could sue?

A grin this time, a scraper raised in her honor. She wiggled her fingers in a little hello, took another sip of her tea to introduce the concept of moisture back into her throat and hummed a musical number.

Hello my baby, hello my honey, hello my fan-ta-sy…

She thought maybe he'd make a good corporate executive and she the CEO of a company threatened by his hostile takeover…

Except, wait, hang on, hold it, stop right there.

She was twenty-six, she was female, she was straight, she was single, she had money in the bank, and now that the dark days were behind her, for once not a care in the world.

And not a single, solitary reason to keep herself from making this fantasy come true.

She gulped more tea. Even the thought had shaken her. And then it stopped shaking her and started stirring her instead.

No way. She couldn't. Because…well, obviously, because…

She didn't know why not. She just knew there was a "why not" and it was undoubtedly a good one. A sensible one. One any girl in her right mind should be able to come up with on the spot. Darcy's mind was too clouded by hormones and the giddy excitement of being launched out of grief and drudgery and servitude and out of a stale, stagnant relationship into the world of new male possibilities.

Molly. She needed to call Molly, her best friend from the day they'd met at Longfellow Middle School in sixth grade. Molly was sensible, practical, down-to-earth and had been a Rock of Gibraltar and a pillar and an Atlas in Darcy's world for years while it persisted in falling apart. A few sane words from Molly and the "why not" would be perfectly obvious to the point where Darcy would be embarrassed to have had the idea in the first place.

So.

She got up from her chaise and sauntered past Garrett's ladder into the house—she'd be talked out of the idea of seduction soon enough, so why not have a little saunter-ish fun in the meantime?—aware his eyes were on her.

Well, she hoped his eyes were on her. She wasn't crass enough to check. In her mind his eyes were glued to her body and radiated approval over every female part. And then some.

Inside, she grabbed her cell from the top of the bookcase in the kitchen that still housed her mother's one hundred and forty-seven cookbooks, maybe three of which her father and she had cracked open after Mom died, and dialed.

"Hey, Molly."

"Do you not *love* this weather? You can count on Wisconsin to come up with a day or two of spring a mere two months after the season has started."

"Then straight into heat waves."

"Uh-huh. What's doing? I hear a problem in your voice."

Darcy smiled. Could a man and woman ever get this close? She didn't think so. In her opinion sisters and best girlfriends had the stronger connection. "I could use some advice, yeah. There's this guy…"

"Ooh, let me sit for this one—" the sound of a scraping chair "—I'm listening."

"He's painting my house."

"And?"

"I…want him." She could see his legs if she stood next to the sink and peered out her kitchen window. She even wanted his legs.

"And you're calling me because…"

"Talk me out of it."

"Uh-oh. Out of what? Hang on—Kyle, for God's sake, have I not said this a hundred times? You can have those *after* dinner. You want something now, have raisins or a banana, and don't 'oh, Mom' me. You'll thank me when you're eighty and still have your teeth and a reasonable waistline—I'm back, Darce. Talk you out of what?"

"Seducing him."

"Sed—are you out of your *mind?*"

Darcy recoiled from Molly's uncharacteristic near-shriek. "I'm calling you, so not quite yet, no. Tell me. Why is it a bad idea?"

"You can't think of any reason?"

"Mmm, no." She sighed over his ankles, shins and thighs. "Not one."

"Honestly. For starters, he could be a psychopath, sociopath serial killer—"

"True." Though odds heavily favored otherwise.

"—or have horrible diseases—"

"Ew. True." Her glorious swelling fantasy deflated a bit.

"—or he could turn out to be one of those stalkers who can't let a girl alone after he's had her once, like what happened to Jody—"

"Oooh, true." She cringed, remembering the hell their friend Jody had gone through after one date with a guy she'd met on MySpace. Police had been involved. 'Nuff said.

See? Calling Molly had been a good idea.

"—or he could be one of those vain, cocky guys who'll get vainer and more cocky after you land him, and brag to his friends that he got laid on the job by some lonely single chick—"

"Blech. Ptooey." Darcy made a face like a child given nasty medicine. Fantasy leaking serious air now.

"Or he could be a nice guy who would like you as you really are—a smart, sweet, nice girl—and would be turned off by you initiating sex when you don't even know him. You could ruin a really good thing that was otherwise meant to be."

Darcy's nasty-medicine face smoothed. Now Molly was sounding like her father. And as much as Darcy had adored her father, nothing made her immediately want to be a teenage rebel again more than someone sounding like him.

She'd spent her life as a good girl because Dad refused to have it any other way. The one time she'd tried to express a little of the devil in her with a low-cut, ooh-la-la outfit she'd bought on the sly and sneaked on in the girls' room before school's opening bell, her father had found out. Hunky Evan Jacobus had practically drooled on the floor that day at school and the next, when she'd worn another very-unlike-her ensemble she'd borrowed from Tiffany Blatz. Darcy had gulped the male attention like a famine victim's first meal. See? She wasn't invisible to the opposite gender, after all.

Evan had even come over that night unexpectedly "to study" and had seen her in her regular appease-daddy clothes, and right in front of her father a question had risen from the murky depths of his teenage brain and emerged from his thin chapped lips. How come she'd been dressing so differently at school?

Daddy had not been amused. Evan didn't stay long. The clothes were given away to those more fortunate than Darcy.

And then there was Greg whom she'd met at a Summerfest concert before senior year at University of Wisconsin Milwaukee, jealous streak a mile wide, threatened by his fifteen-year head start on life. He'd wanted Darcy to look sexy only in the privacy of his or her bedroom, which hadn't been often enough for her taste. But from his perspective, guys her age were everywhere and Greg didn't want them looking and he didn't want her to see them looking and, and, and…

Darcy's fantasy started to reinflate. "I don't know. I still—"

"Look, Darce, I know how much you need to feel you're breaking out of the mode you've been in. You've had some really tough years and made a lot of sacrifices that took a lot of strength. But selling the house and spending the next eight years moving around the country is plenty adventurous, though I think you don't realize how much you're leaving here."

Darcy rolled her eyes. "Can we save that lecture for another time? I don't need that one today."

"Yes. Okay. Hang on—Annabel, I told you to get ready for gymnastics *ten minutes ago* and you haven't even started changing. *Go.* I'm back, Darce. Man, that girl is going to turn my hair white and she's only four. What was I saying, now?"

"About me cutting loose."

"Right. Let's face it, Greg was about as exciting as a PTA meeting, and you—"

"Hey," Darcy protested automatically, then frowned. Molly wasn't usually this cutting. Or this impatient with her children.

"Why else did you break up with him? I'm right. You know I am."

"Yes, but only I'm allowed to slam him."

"Okay. How about, 'Mr. Gregory Hinshaw did not encourage you to explore your own life.' Better?"

"Much." Greg had been gentle, wonderful, but yeah, set in his ways was an understatement. Cemented in his ways, maybe. "That works."

"So the point is, don't go overboard now that you're free. Remember, the kids in college who partied their brains out and ended up puking in the street every weekend were the ones whose parents absolutely forbade them to touch alcohol. Ever."

Darcy tapped her fingers on the rim of the sink. "I get it, Molly."

"I'm just saying. I don't want you to do something so out of character that you'll wish you hadn't."

"But it can't be completely out of character or why would I want to do it?"

"Because you've been bent too far in one direction, and now that pressure is released, you're whipping too far over to the other side. Trust me. You want danger? Throw out a recyclable, or park in a handicapped space—something more in your risk league. Leave seducing strangers to women who can handle the fallout."

Darcy growled loudly. Now Molly sounded like Dad *and* Greg. In stereo. Full volume. And unfortunately, even though she might be making perfect sense, out of sheer contrariness Darcy's desire to make use of Garrett's mighty spear tripled.

"Hey, you wanted me to talk you out of it."

"Yeah, I did. I did want you to talk me out of it." The legs in her kitchen window moved down a step. Darcy leaned over the sink to better admire their straight muscled length, raising her eyes slowly to where he kept the weaponry she was "soooo uncharacteristically" in the mood to test out. "But I'm pretty sure I just changed my mind."

2

TYLER HOUSTON finished sanding the upper sill of a second-story window, climbed down and moved the ladder to the last one on that floor. For the third day in a row he'd lingered here after the other guys had gone. Partly because rather than being a professional painter like his coworkers, he was a soon-to-be college professor—and yes, he did like the sound of that—earning extra cash over the summer before he started teaching economics at UWM in the fall. The guys kidded him about his snail-speed painting, but after so many years of book study it was a refreshing break to work with his body again instead of just his mind.

As he'd said, that was partly why he stayed late. To catch up. But only partly.

The other "partly" had to do with the woman this house belonged to. He'd been attracted to plenty of women in his life. Some based purely on appearance, seen at a distance or seen up close. Some whose personality appealed and whose looks seemed to morph into loveliness the more he got to know them. But rarely the kind of punch-to-the-gut sizzle he experienced with this woman. Even his attraction to Annie Phillips, his supposed-to-be fiancée who'd busted his heart wide open a year ago, had taken hold of him slowly.

Hardly Mr. Smooth, he still could generally hold his end up in a conversation. He liked people, enjoyed finding out about them, listening to their stories, figuring out what made them tick. Around this woman, he'd been able only to comment moronically about paint. Compliment her color choice. Admire her house. Wax philosophical about wood stain and window glazing. Never even asked her name. Worse, he'd kept laughing nervously—he would not use the term giggle. Bad enough when she had on her sunglasses, but when she took them off and looked at him with those blue-gray eyes…

Of course she'd been completely cool, able to look at him directly, to speak coherently without giggling—er, nervous laughter. Periodically she'd toss her heavy dark hair back as if it annoyed her by continually creeping over her shoulders. Even that was sexy to him.

Earlier today, warmer even than yesterday once the cloud cover passed on to the east, she'd been sitting in her usual lounge chair—in jeans and a large man's shirt that made him jealous of whoever had given it to her—reading a book and listening to an iPod. He'd managed to avoid looking at her for the most part, but his gaze was jerked over when she'd sat up abruptly, put the book down and started unbuttoning the shirt.

That got his attention. Then the shirt was tossed aside and he nearly gouged the wood of the sill he was scraping when she hiked up the tight, fiery-orange-red top underneath, yanked it over her head and flung it to the side as if it harbored bees.

While his tongue had lolled out of his mouth—figuratively speaking—she'd calmly picked up her book and settled back down.

He'd worked particularly slowly after that, at least until she disappeared back into the house a while earlier. Because underneath she wore a bikini top that she filled out like…like…

Poetic words failed him. "Like beautiful breasts in a bikini top," was about as lyrical a description as he could manage.

Clearly he'd gone over the edge. Next he'd be like Katie,

his younger sister, who claimed to have known the second she met Edwin, now her husband of two years, that he was the love of her life.

Uh-huh.

If Tyler were a different kind of scientist, he'd do research into why and how two people could produce such sparks. Or rather how one person could produce them in another, since he had no way of knowing if the ones he felt were reciprocated.

He started scraping the final window to what must be her bedroom, the sun still out but the air rapidly cooling toward evening. The last few days had been warm, though Milwaukee hung on to chilly nights until close to the start of summer. Last month he'd moved back here to his hometown and only a block away from Ms. Bikini in order to—

The corner of his eye caught movement beyond the old-fashioned slightly wavy glass.

Her. Coming into her bedroom. What was her name? He was dying to know. Something sexy and slightly old-fashioned, like Rosemary. She walked in and passed the window, still in those jeans, low-cut and tight, still in that bikini top, again under the man's shirt, which flared open when she moved and which continued to make him jealous. Who had given it to her? Was she still involved with him?

Tyler really needed to pay attention to this window or he'd be here all night. And not the way he'd like to be, in Rosemary's…er, company, but out here standing on a ladder with only a scraper for intimacy.

So he paid attention to the window. He really did. But his peripheral vision was working, too, and kept track of her. Then he had to glance right at her just once, to confirm if what he thought he'd seen was in fact what he thought he'd seen.

Because what he thought he'd seen was her shirt fluttering to the floor.

Yes.

The shirt.

On the floor.

Worse—no, better—no, worse—her hands were now at the fastenings of her jeans. He scraped extra loud, making sure his knuckles rapped "clumsily" on the glass so she'd realize he was there and that he could…

Her jeans traveled down long, long, strong legs, one of which stepped out of them, followed by the other.

…see. He could see. He could do nothing but see. Dark wavy hair streaming down to her collarbone, skin a light shade of gold, broad shoulders, slender waist, toned ass…

Her hands reached around to the back hook of her bathing suit top.

Ho-ly sh—

Wait. He was not behaving like the gentleman his mother had raised.

"Hey." He tapped on the window. No reaction. He tapped harder. *"Hey."*

How could she possibly not know he was there? He didn't see any earbuds or the cord of an iPod. She must be able to hear him knocking. She must know he was there.

The bikini top slid to the ground. Which meant…

She knew he was there.

He put the scraper down on the sill. Tyler had never been like his late older brother Cam, whom women tried to seduce at various times, like, oh, say, whenever he was awake. If this was business as usual for painters, maybe Tyler should switch careers. Though he hadn't gotten this…uh, lucky when he'd painted houses in college.

Maybe because he'd never painted for anyone like Rosemary before. Not just beauty, not just body, something else. A familiarity, a sense that he knew her even having just met her. Knew she was a good person, knew he could trust her, knew they had things in common. How could he possibly know any of that? He couldn't. He was projecting. The connection was purely physical, animal, primal. Her hormones fit his, her pheromones broadcasted to his frequency, her…uh…her…

…breasts, God, her breasts. Naked, they tilted, slid, hung lushly as she bent to pick up her top. His throat became dry. She tossed her hair, arched her back, slid her hands up her stomach to cup, then cover, then caress them.

His throat became drier. Desert dry. His cock swelled. He wanted to touch her more than he'd ever wanted anything in his life. If he wasn't put off by the concept of deep, possibly fatal lacerations from broken glass, he'd dive through her window and ravish her.

She swayed dreamily to some inner music, fingering her nipples, smile curving her lips, her body in profile. She still hadn't looked at him. He still hadn't looked away.

Her hips started to move, small, then larger circles. He let out a deep helpless groan he hadn't been planning to let out. He wanted to grab hold of his dictator dick, which was ordering in no uncertain terms that its pain be relieved in whatever way possible, preferably in some way involving the wonder that was Rosemary.

Her hands left her breasts, which suited him fine. The easier to see her with, my dear, and the view was spectacular. Except then her hands took a trip to the sides of her bikini bottoms and began to edge them down, one side a fraction of an inch, then the other, as her hips continued their 'round and 'round and back and forth and forward and back journey, a journey he wanted desperately to join them on because he knew what destination they'd lead him to.

The bikini slid the last several smooth inches down her thighs, knees, calves, ankles and hit the floor. She turned and faced him, making direct eye contact through the glass. Well…eventual direct eye contact. His eyes were busy briefly before they made it up to hers. He was a guy, he couldn't help it.

Silence. Stillness. Emotions swirling in him—desire, and something softer, like tenderness, which he didn't understand, hadn't felt for anyone since Annie, and not even for her this soon after they'd met.

The scraper chose that moment to slide off the uneven stone sill and clatter to the ground. He didn't blame it. There wasn't much holding him up, either—with the exception of the obvious, which had no trouble standing straight and proud.

Now what?

Okay, he wasn't *that* lame. He knew what. But should he? He was working here; he was her employee in a sense. Maybe she was one of those women who seduced then cried rape. A charge like that could ruin his career.

But he knew she wasn't. How? He didn't know. He knew being with her would be carnal and exciting and sweet all at the same time, and he didn't know how he knew that, either.

He also didn't know how he was going to face his sister, who'd said all these same stupid and illogical things about her husband hours after they'd met, which had precipitated the most bitter fight he and Katie had ever had as siblings, one that worsened when she'd eloped and one from which they still hadn't recovered, to both their sadness. But so far, not regret.

His feet seemed to have decided what to do, or maybe it was that other part of him. He nodded at Rosemary and climbed down the ladder, suddenly aware of his less-than-fresh condition, having rolled out of bed at the last possible second into his clothes and a cup of coffee to stand in the sun all day.

Ripe, to say the least.

Still led by his feet or maybe the part that stuck out the farthest and felt the most eager, he found her back door unlocked, found the oak staircase and climbed toward heaven.

At the doorway to her room, he stopped. A double room, a master bedroom suite in addition to the other two bedrooms he'd glimpsed. Unusual for these old houses, which usually fit only two bedrooms upstairs. Beautiful room, hardwood floors, decorative molding and thick solid doors. She'd decorated in a way that suited his taste—dark wood furniture, classic prints on the walls, colorful rugs, subdued rose-beige walls—nothing too modern or too girlie.

That analysis took him all of five seconds, which was all he was willing to dedicate to the decor. The woman interested him far more.

He walked through the outer room and paused at the arched entrance to her bedroom. She lay on the king-size bed, modestly covered by a sheet, expression slightly apprehensive, which put him at ease. If she was nervous then she wasn't a habitual man-eater.

"Hi." He grinned. He couldn't help it, but at least he didn't giggle. "You, uh, caught my eye in here."

She laughed, which he liked. Not nervously, but as if she understood and enjoyed his understatement. "Noticed me, did you?"

"I don't think I've noticed anything quite that much in a long time."

"Mmm, really?"

"Mmm, really." He moved forward until his thighs in their shorts rested against the bottoms of her feet. Now she even looked familiar. Had he seen her before? But there'd been no moment of recognition when he'd first set eyes on her three days earlier. "I was wondering…"

"Yes?"

"If there was something you needed my help doing."

Her eyes stayed on his, her hand pushed up into her hair as she adjusted her head on the pillow. "There is, yes."

"What's that?" He reached down, rested his hands lightly on her ankles.

"I want to come."

Sexual adrenaline surged. He made himself look calm. "And you don't want to do that alone?"

"Not this time, no."

"Hmm." He pretended to consider. "You know, I think I can help you."

The touch of shyness in her smile pierced him. "I thought maybe you could."

"But…I could use a shower first."

"Oh." She bunched her lips as if trying to tolerate pain. "I'm not sure I can wait that long."

He gave her foot an affectionate squeeze. "Trust me, you'll be happier if I'm clean."

"Yes. Okay." She let out a long sigh of near despair. "Bathroom's to the right and straight ahead. Clean towels in the closet next to it. And, Garrett?"

"Garrett?"

"My name for you. It means 'with a mighty spear.'"

He laughed—nervously. Though mighty was open to interpretation. "Yes, Rosemary."

"Rosemary?"

"Mine for you." He realized she was waiting expectantly. "It means Rose…Mary."

Her brief laughter turned into the smile that was way too fast becoming familiar and dear to him. "Good enough. Now go. And don't forget to come back. This is my first-ever seduction and I want to make sure it happens."

He nodded and left the room before his latest ridiculous

surge of emotion became visible. He was her first. God, he needed to get a grip.

Showering at the speed of light wasn't humanly possible, but his didn't happen much slower. He didn't bother putting his sweaty paint-smelling clothes back on but wrapped the thick, generous towel around his waist. A glance in the mirror, wondering what the hell she saw in what he'd always considered average looks and build. Maybe she considered him a sure thing for her first attempt at seduction, given how much virtual drooling he'd done over her?

He'd rather think there was something powerful and exciting between them. Which would most likely get more powerful and more exciting in the very near future.

The hardwood creaked under his feet in that comforting way of old houses, to remind those inside not to forget their surroundings.

"Hi." Rosemary sounded shy again.

"I'm clean."

"So you are." One dark brow arched briefly. "While I am still feeling pretty dirty."

He knelt on the edge of the bed then stretched out beside her, no longer nervous, thank God, though he usually was the first time with someone, certainly had been a wreck with Annie. "I promised to help you with that. And I will."

"Very grateful." She lay on her side, facing him, both hands under her cheek. "I was serious when I said I've never done this before."

"Had sex with a stranger?"

"I did that once. In college. But I was drunk and he was, too, and I bet neither of us remembers much about it. Probably just as well." She considered him thoughtfully. "It's funny, you don't seem like a stranger. But I'm sure I don't know you."

"I'm *sure* I'd remember you."

"Thank you." She blushed and lowered her eyes, which made an unbearably appealing contrast to her boldness. "I meant, I've never taken the initiative like this with someone I didn't know."

"And?"

She shrugged. "So far, so good. You haven't killed me."

"Trust me, that's the furthest thing from my mind." He touched her hair, stroked it off her face, down the back of her head, over her shoulders and onto the bare skin of her back under the cool cotton sheet, stroked there, up and down, easing any tension with his fingers. "But if anything feels wrong at any point, tell me. You don't have to do this."

"Mmm, I definitely do. I like the way you touch me." She arched into his fingers, stretched her long, beautiful spine.

"This is only the beginning of how I want to touch you." His voice came out lower and more earnestly than he meant it to. He reached farther, to the curve of her lower back, then dared a slow glide over her firm shapely rear, which not only brought a sexy "Mmm" out of her, but also made her squirm closer and start her soft graceful hands on an exploration of their own. Of him.

Taking this as slowly as he wanted to might result in his death.

He tugged the sheet off her and pulled her flush against him, pressing his erection rhythmically against her, making sure he was stimulating her where it did the most good, tormenting himself in the sweetest possible way. Then he gathered her thick hair between his fingers, traced his thumbs along her jaw and did what he'd wanted to do since seeing her the first time. He kissed her full, tempting mouth.

The connection was immediate and electric, traveling through their lips, down his body, taking him over. He kissed her again and again, rolled her impatiently onto her back and followed to cover her, still tasting and fitting their lips together at every possible angle until the waves of eroticism and some other nameless feeling were so strong he had to stop.

He drew back slightly, breathing hard, feeling awed, met the awe in her eyes and became aware of the heaving rhythm of her breath, too. Both. They both felt it.

"Whoa." She clasped her hands behind his neck and laughed uncertainly. "I guess I picked you for a reason."

"Fate." He didn't believe in fate or any of the woo-woo crap that dominated his sister's world, but the second he said the word he felt it was true.

Her eyes became cautious and he made himself grin to show he was kidding. Ha, ha. Fate. Ha, ha.

What the *hell* was the matter with him? He was a very practical down-to-earth guy who viewed the world in practical and often purely scientific terms.

"Oh, um, here." She rummaged under the pillow and came up with a row of condoms, each in its black foil package. Speaking of practical. "I wasn't sure if you'd be prepared so I made sure I was."

"You planned well." He lifted off her and took the strip.

"Only since yesterday." She watched him open a packet. "I was lying on the lawn and fantasizing about you, and then I thought why not?"

"Why not?" He rolled on the condom then dragged his finger in a slow zigzag down from her neck, spiraling up each breast, meandering over her stomach and gently parting the lips of her sex. Her eyes closed and he watched her face, his fingers traveling by instinct, by touch, manipulating her softness, dipping into the tight entrance for moisture, spreading it outward again and again until her clit was slippery and firm.

Her head lifted from the pillow then sank, lashes dark on her cheek, a frown of concentration forming a furrow between her brows. It hit him that he would still want to know her when time had made the furrow permanent, would still want to be here touching her, watching the flush bloom on her face and her lips part. He'd tried to picture himself and Annie old together even up until the day he asked her to marry him, but it hadn't seemed possible they'd ever be anything but young.

He moved over Rosemary, spread her legs gently. Her eyes opened and he sank not only into her body but almost as blissfully into her gaze before he began a slow rhythm. She joined it and he was quite sure he had known her a long time and would know her a lot longer, that they'd make love like this many, many times and it would always be this exciting, hot and sweet.

His cheek found hers; he listened to her breath speed and slow, felt her body eventually starting to strain toward her climax. Sliding his hands under her, he tilted her pelvis up, raised himself slightly, increased his pace and heard her low moan with satisfaction. Pleasing her was all he cared about right now, giving her what she'd asked from him. Then he wanted to give her a lot more than that.

Her eyes closed; her hands scrabbled across the sheets. She gripped them and her hips pushed up hard. He bit his lip, willing himself to wait…wait…wait…

And then her eyes shot wide; her head lifted, mouth opened in a silent "Oh," and he felt her build, hold and go over. He fought against his own orgasm as long as he could stand it, savoring their connection, wanting this time to last forever. She gave a beautiful satisfied moan, whispered something he only barely caught about how perfectly he filled her and how much she loved feeling him inside her, and his control was gone. His climax burst out like a horse from a starting gate, a deep, shuddering release that went on and on and on. In the middle of such perfect ecstasy as he strained against her, trying to keep her closer than was physically possible, it occurred to him that he loved her and would always love her and somehow had always loved her.

She let her hands fall to the side, smile on her lips, flush on her cheeks, and stretched beneath him. Her breathing slowed gradually. Her smile stayed in place. She opened her eyes and he was stunned by their warmth and glow. His love. His one and only love.

Then she blinked.

"Hot damn. That orgasm nearly took my head off." She grinned at him, apparently completely in control of herself and her emotions. "Was that not fabulous?"

"It was." His voice was husky; he felt dazed and stupid. "Fabulous."

"Whew. I definitely picked the right guy." She moved as if she wanted him off her, so he rolled to one side, spent and confused. "Want a glass of water? I'm parched."

"Sure. Yeah." He sat up, nodding his thanks when she tossed him a box of tissues.

"Man." She took a couple of bowlegged steps and laughed. "I can barely walk. You are incredible."

Right. Incredible. Totally. Stud of the month, in fact. He yanked out a couple of tissues, went to the bathroom to get rid of the condom and clean himself up, then got dressed in the paint-and-perspiration-smelling clothes he'd shed with such anticipation.

So he'd given her what she wanted—an orgasm that nearly took her head off. While he'd gotten something he didn't want at all. A heart about as vulnerable as it had ever been, in a ridiculously short time frame. In all the years of dating Annie he didn't think he'd ever felt this raw and open. At least not until she dumped him.

As soon as he was dressed, had his glass of water and said goodbye, he was out of there, taking his suddenly foolish and sentimental heart with him.

Because he really wasn't into having it stomped on again.

3

DARCY POSITIVELY FLOATED through her house. She kept laughing for no reason, drifting into one room, looking around hardly seeing a thing, frowning, hands on her hips, then laughing again and tilting into another room, whirling in a circle as if she'd gone completely over the edge.

Maybe she had. No, she'd done something much better. Last night she'd achieved a state of total—okay, *near* total—confidence and had walked into the master bedroom, knowing "Garrett" was working at her window, able to see everything. And in spite of the fact that her hands were shaking a little and once in a while she could barely draw a breath, she'd shown him…everything.

Could the evening have been any more perfect? No, and no, and no again.

He'd been a wonderful lover. Not that she had so many to compare him to, but she couldn't usually come the first time with someone and…wow. Well. She had. Almost twice, but the second one had surprised her so much she'd ruined it by paying too much attention. Like when you were about to sneeze, if you thought too hard about it, the urge stopped.

Not only a wonderful lover, he'd been sweet. Gentle. And when he looked deeply into her eyes and kissed her…

Well, never mind. This wasn't about falling in love or wildly inappropriate degrees of emotionalism, considering she knew nothing about him except he was a painter. And very considerate. And handsome in a non-obvious way and sexy as hell and sort of familiar in that way strangers were sometimes.

After, in case he thought she was the kind of idiot who fell for every guy she slept with, she'd made sure not to act as clingy and vulnerable as she felt. Thank God, because he'd left the microsecond he could, as if he had rockets in his shoes. Obviously he didn't consider last night the beginning of a beautiful friendship. Which was fine. What she wanted, actually. After the paint job was over she'd never see him again. The whole thing would be just as neat and tidy as she'd planned it.

She tried to dance into the dining room but her body didn't feel much like dancing all of a sudden. Maybe she was feeling wistful over him because he was her virgin seduction and she'd always have a soft spot for the experience. And for him. Understandable, really, and not based on anything but him being her first fantasy-come-true. She'd been so sensible through her relationship with Greg and this had been so wild and—

No, not really that wild. Carnal, sure, but sweetly carnal if such a thing were possible. Tender almost. Lovely. He'd wanted to shower instead of hop on immediately and ride his way to oblivion. Consideration for her; she'd liked that a lot. Not to mention the smell of her favorite vanilla soap on his skin had been quite the aphrodisiac. But it was the look in his eyes and that odd déjà vu feeling that had really touched her in a deep place she—

Anyway, enough of that. She wanted to call Molly and find some way to trumpet her success without any told-you-so triumph since Garrett hadn't turned out to be a diseased-stalker-serial-killer, but it was way too early, just after 6 a.m. Darcy was usually a late sleeper but adrenaline had woken her with the dawn this morning after a fitful sleep. She'd call Molly later, after Molly had gotten her kids to preschool and Bruce to work. Right now Darcy had better remember she was still on planet

earth and get busy. There were plenty of her family's posses-
sions to go through and get rid of before the house sold. Some
had already been doled out to Dad's relatives. The things Darcy
wanted were moved into long-term storage, ready for her own
place, wherever and whenever she chose to settle down.

An hour later she'd gone through her dad's study, occasionally weepy, mostly stoic, and made piles—give away, sell, toss.
She'd paused over a painting of a ship on Lake Michigan for
quite a while. Derek Houston had painted it for Dad probably
a quarter century ago. For decades Derek was their backyard
neighbor over on 64th Street. He'd died some years ago, but
his widow, Marjory, still lived there, or had last spring, last time
Darcy had been around. Confidentially, Darcy hated the bright
surreal colors and crooked lines, but she hated to give the
painting away even more, since her dad had loved it so much.
Derek's widow should have it back.

She glanced at the clock. Seven-thirty. Marjory would be up
by now. When Darcy was a girl out of bed for school at six-
thirty every morning, bleary-eyed and annoyed at the hour,
she'd seen her neighbor drinking coffee in her yard, watching
birds at her feeder even on the coldest mornings. Darcy could
take the painting to her right now. One less thing to do later.

With the canvas carefully swaddled in enough bubble wrap
to protect an empty robin's egg, Darcy took the shortcut,
pushing through the arbor vitae that Dad had planted ten years
earlier at the back of the yard for privacy, now a thick tall row
of sentry trees. The painting she lifted over the back fence then
dropped gently to the ground, and followed with a quick climb
over. A jump and she was in the Houstons' yard, then on their
driveway, remembering other climbs here to retrieve over en-
thusiastically tossed balls or Frisbees.

Marjory Houston had been wonderful when Dad was in bad
shape before Darcy moved him to the hospice. She'd baked

cookies to tempt his appetite when he started losing so much weight, offered to stay with him now and then so Darcy could get some relief. Darcy felt guilty that during the past year spent in Madison to be closer to Greg, she hadn't visited or called to see if Marjory needed anything.

The last twelve months had been a strange combination of selfless and selfish. Selfless because she'd stayed to help Greg through the long painful struggle back to his old self, physically and mentally, even though she'd wanted out of the relationship. And selfish because she'd spent too much time in self-pity and resentment, and stopped nurturing friends and therefore herself.

She stepped up the brick steps of Marjory's walkway, grinning at the stone lions pompously posed atop waist-high brick columns on either side, as if Marjory lived in Versailles and not a typical Midwestern bungalow. It would be good to see her. A slice of Darcy's childhood, precious for still being around.

The doorbell echoed through the house. Was she home?

She was. Footsteps, then the door swung open and—

So did Darcy's mouth.

"Hi." He was obviously very surprised to see her, but not nearly as very surprised as she was to see him. "Good morning."

"What are you doing here?"

He looked taken aback. "I live here."

"*You* live here?"

"I think that's what I just said." His eyes crinkled at the corners when he smiled. Somehow she'd forgotten that or hadn't noticed and now she was even more flustered because it was extremely sexy.

"Where is Marjory?"

"Ah. Marjory." His smile dimmed. "She had a stroke. We had to put her in an assisted-living facility."

"Oh, no." She hugged the painting to her, feeling even more

guilty now for not keeping up with her neighbor and friend, staring at the last person she'd expected to see. Then something he said penetrated.

"*You* put her in an assisted-living facility?"

"I'm her great-nephew." Then he stuck out his hand as if they hadn't spent the previous night sweating and straining toward gigantic climaxes together, but were meeting for the first time. "Tyler Houston."

Oh, my Lord. *Tyler Houston.* Big brother of Katie, her erstwhile track teammate, and awkward little brother of Cameron Houston. Cam was every schoolgirl's bad-boy dream come true; true to form, he'd met a wasteful and tragic end in early adulthood. No wonder Tyler had looked familiar. Trust Darcy to think that sense of déjà vu was some sign from the universe rather than the simple fact that she actually did know him. Vaguely anyway.

"I'm…" She took one hand away from the bubble-wrapped painting to shake his, and her perspiring skin made an embarrassing sucking-tearing sound as it separated from the plastic. "Darcy Wolf."

"Wow. Darcy Wolf." He shook her hand, staring at her as if she were the big bad one. Then he dropped his arm and chuckled, but not as if something were funny in a good way.

She was pretty sure she knew what he was thinking. Both of them had gone into last night as a fantasy, the chance to leave behind their real identities and follow a powerful attraction to its passionate conclusion without baggage or expectations.

Now it turned out they had a shared past, more parallel than intertwined, but related certainly. There were many people Darcy didn't want to find out that she'd stripped to seduce a workman at her house, and he would know a lot of them. In fact, Molly's husband, Bruce, was a distant cousin of his.

She'd bet Tyler was about as happy to discover who she was as she was to discover who he was. Namely: not.

"Well." She could feel herself blushing and stupidly clutched the painting harder as if she could cool her face that way. At least she'd told no-longer-Garrett that he was her first seduction, so he couldn't tell anyone she probably made getting naked for strangers a habit. On the other hand, he might be enough of a gentleman not to tell anyone at all. That would be nice. "Tyler Houston. Imagine that. Ha."

Her intense discomfort amused him apparently. Or something did. "Come on in. I don't have to leave for your house for another fifteen minutes. The coffee's still hot and I have a blueberry cake that should be finished."

"Oh, you know...I just wanted to drop this off for Marjory." She held out her ludicrously padded package, feeling a panicked need to run from this complete reconfiguration of her last twelve hours so she could think the new version through. "It's a painting. By Mr. Hous...uh, your great-uncle. I wanted Marjory to have it back."

"Thanks." He took the painting. "You don't want to keep it? I'm sure she wouldn't mind."

"Oh. Well." She moved her hair back behind her shoulders, where it never wanted to stay, desperately trying to think of some reason not to keep the artwork other than loathing. "I'm just...I... Well, she should have it."

He winked and she felt a little fizzy in response. "I didn't like his work, either. But Aunt Marjory was proud of him. She'll appreciate this, thank you."

"My dad loved the painting. He hung it in his study, over his desk."

"That's nice to know." His eyes warmed with sympathy and her fizz got fizzier. "I heard about your dad last year. I'm sorry."

"Thank you. I miss him, but I'm glad he's at peace now."

"I can't believe I didn't figure out who you were. I assumed the house had been sold by now and that you were the new owner."

"No. The old one." She took a step back, frantic to escape. This was horrible. How did you have a polite catching-up conversation with someone as if you hadn't seen him in years, when last night…

"Sure you won't have coffee?"

"No. No. No, thanks." She grimaced. Think she could say no a few more times?

"Okay." His eyes cooled. "See you later."

"Uh. I'm probably going to be out most of the day."

"Right." His lips scrunched into a line; he turned back into his house, lifting his hand. "Bye."

Darcy nodded idiotically at the back of his head, then turned and fled up 64th Street, not feeling entitled to the shortcut anymore. She turned right on Clarke, south on 63rd, into her house and directly to her phone, desperately needing Molly.

"Good morning, sunshine."

"Hi, Molly. Um…I need to…Last night…"

"Uh-oh, crisis." Molly sighed. "I had three already this morning. Can't find favorite shirt, didn't like breakfast, left shoes across the street at Ricky's house."

"Sorry, I know you're swamped."

"For you, I can handle it. Just don't call me Mom or honey."

"Deal."

"So?"

Darcy wrinkled her nose and launched herself into furious back-and-forth pacing across the now-rugless hardwood floor in the living room. "Last night. You know that painter I told you about?"

"Uh-oh. You did it…or rather, you did him?"

"Yes."

"And now begins the fallout. Won't say I-told-you-so, but want to."

"No, last night was fine. More than fine. Perfect. He was…"

She stopped pacing, unable to tell her best friend, whom she told absolutely everything, any details. "Well, it was perfect."

"I'm getting the perfect part, but you're not in crisis over that."

"No. So. This morning, I go to Marjory Houston's house to take back one of her husband's paintings."

"The hideous one from your dad's study?"

"Yup. Only it's not Marjory Houston at the house."

"No, she's at Royal Oaks."

"Instead it's… Well, it's…"

"Tyler Houston lives there now."

"Right. Him."

"And?"

"Him, Molly. *Him.*"

Molly's gasp came over the line loud and clear, followed by a giggle. "Oh. My. God. You seduced Tyler Houston?"

"Apparently."

Molly of course only saw the humor in this disaster and helped herself to a good long belly laugh at Darcy's expense. "You didn't recognize him?"

"Why would I? I only saw him a few times that I can remember, and that was over ten years ago. He's at least five years older than me, and let's face it, sort of invisible next to his brother."

"But you can see him now, I take it."

"He grew up." She pictured him coming into her room naked except for the towel and then naked without the towel and couldn't help a dreamy smile. If only he'd stayed Garrett. But even now, knowing he was Tyler didn't change that last night was perfect.

"So what now? When are you going to see him next?"

"I'm not." She started pacing again. "Obviously."

"What? Why?"

"Because it was only an accident that he turned out to be a real person. While he was a fantasy, the entire experience was amazing."

"Oh, give me a—"

"I'm serious." She directed her pacing to the ugly brown couch by the front window and sprawled on it. "And I want more."

"You just said you weren't going to see him."

"No. With someone else. A different fantasy. Last night was amazing, Molly. I felt so free and powerful. And sexy, like movie-star sexy. The most amazing high I've ever had. I want that again."

"Okay, now you're scaring me."

"No. I'm telling you, it was incredible."

"Yeah, I hear heroin gives a pretty good high, too. Doesn't make it a good idea."

"Honestly." Darcy gave a boring beige throw pillow a good solid punch. "Do all people start parenting everyone they know after they have kids?"

"Only when they need it."

"Molly…"

"You know, the more I think about it, you and Tyler could make a really good couple. He's smart, funny, really sharp. He'll be teaching at UWM next fall. Bruce admires him, and you know Bruce, he doesn't suffer fools."

"I know that about Bruce."

"So why not? Is he interested? I mean, obviously he was last night. What guy wouldn't be with your, er, charming offer on the table. But this morning?"

Darcy scrunched up her mouth. He had looked at her sort of eagerly now that she thought about it. He had invited her in for coffee. Her insides started to warm and soften. His eyes were such a gorgeous color. Sometimes blue, sometimes green, often both. They made her—

Wait, what was she thinking? "Whether or not he's interested is beside the point. I'm not interested."

"Why not? He's a hell of a catch."

"I'm leaving town in a few weeks. Why would I want to start something? The only thing I have room for is fun."

"Right." Molly made a characteristic scoffing sound and Darcy could picture her disapproving face as if she was in the room next to her. "*So.* Then, uh, tell me, what's your next big fun?"

"Well…" She tipped her head to one side, wondering why Molly had asked the question so oddly. Maybe because she didn't really want to know? But Darcy did. What other fantasy could she fulfill? Another of her favorites popped into her head as if it had been waiting impatiently for its turn. "Next I'm going to dress in a sexy, black-leather-mini outfit, stiletto heels, killer makeup and strut into a bar baring my bad-assed attitude for all the world to see."

Molly made a choking sound. "I need antacids just listening to this."

"Aw, c'mon. Haven't you always wanted to be a hot confident babe-ola just for a little while?"

"No, for God's sake, and you know why? Because I have a brain, that's why. Fantasies are called fantasies for a reason, and that reason is this. Because. They're. Not. *Real.*"

Darcy frowned. Not that she expected sensible, practical, anti-glamour Molly, who met Bruce in high school and never looked back, to jump up and down at her idea, but she sounded stretched extra thin and had the day before, too. "Hey, girl. Something's bothering you. What is it?"

"No. Nothing is bothering me."

Darcy let the silence hang. "Moll…"

Molly sighed. "Bruce."

"Bruce…what?"

"He's…started going to some personal trainer." Her sentence accelerated like a sports car. "So what, suddenly he hates the fact that he's getting old and fat when he's been a work in progress for years and years?"

"Bruce is working out?" She tried to picture beefy jolly Bruce breaking a sweat over anything but a Packers game on TV. *"Bruce?"*

"He met this woman through his work, selling her the usual physical therapy equipment. She offers to train him, which she does on the side. He accepts. She's young, stunning, looks like Angelina Jolie. I haven't seen her, this is his description. He talks about her all the time, how great she is, how strong she is, how smart she is…"

"Molly, you've been married eight happy years. Bruce is *not* going to cheat on you. He adores you. I'm sure it's nothing."

"It's a fantasy, Darcy. Fantasies are powerful and they're dangerous. I'm telling you this now, before you get hurt or hurt someone else."

"This is an entirely different situation."

"Right."

Darcy drew down her brows and punched the couch again, torn between annoyance and sympathy. "I'm not out trying to tempt husbands. I just want to have some irresponsible self-indulgent fun for a change."

"Okay, okay. Maybe I'm a little touchy on the subject."

"I understand, I really do. And I would so not worry. Bruce looks at you like you could walk on Lake Michigan."

"Thanks, Darce. I'll try not to." Molly took a deep breath. "So…when are you going to do this hot-babe routine? What bar?"

Again the odd tone. Darcy frowned, not sure whether to call her on it or not, and decided not. "I hadn't really thought that far in advance. But…let's say Saturday. Starlight City. Ten o'clock."

The second she set the date, place and time, everything felt right. She knew she was going to go through with it. She would put the post-fantasy awkwardness with Tyler behind her and march forward, guns blazing, use her newfound powers to reduce Milwaukee's men to quivering mounds of needy testosterone.

"Blech. Starlight City? Total meat market."

"Ya *think?*"

Molly groaned. "Just be careful. Use condoms. Take Mace and pepper spray and a whistle. Don't take him to your house or go to his, find a motel, one of the cheap ones with thin walls so people can hear if you scream. And if you haven't called by midnight Saturday, I'm calling 9-1-1."

"Yes, Mommy."

"Promise?"

She made sure Molly could hear her sigh of exasperation. "Cross my heart and hope to get massively laid."

"Ack! Dear God, I won't live through this."

Darcy giggled. "And, honey, really don't worry about Bruce. He probably just got a wake-up call about his weight and possible health problems and is excited about taking care of himself."

"I hope so, Darce."

"I know so."

She hung up the phone, allowed herself to be one hundred percent sure that Bruce would never cheat on Molly no matter how hot this personal trainer chick was, then grabbed her purse and headed for the garage. The painters would arrive soon, including tempting Tyler, and she was going to visit poor Marjory at Royal Oaks and then…

She had some über-hot black leather to buy.

4

TYLER RODE HIS BICYCLE to a stop outside his garage, swung off and punched in the code to open the door, which squeaked in protest, reminding him that he needed to get out here with some lubricant. He could use some for his legs, too, which were aching; ditto his back and arms. He'd painted windows all day in a state of apprehension, not sure whether he wanted to see Darcy or if he didn't. She never showed, either through the window or outside, which effectively took care of that apprehension but not until the end of the day. By that time he was physically tired but emotionally wired. To exhaust himself further, he'd taken a punishing bike trip up the Little Menomonee River Parkway and back through the city. Barely able to walk now, he still wasn't sure he'd be able to relax.

He didn't like this. His relationship with Annie had been uncomplicated from beginning to end. He'd met her their junior year at Bowdoin College in Maine. They spent time together as friends and then become more. They'd shared a sense of humor, taste in movies, books, food, political views and basic values. In short, they fit together perfectly. Effortlessly.

While Darcy…

Why was he even comparing them? Annie had been his world for years—he'd been sure they'd last a lifetime. This woman he barely knew. And yet, when she'd shown up at his door this morning holding one of Derek Houston's paintings, ludicrously overwrapped, he'd naively assumed she'd been craving him to the same degree he'd been craving her, that she'd gone to endless lengths to find out who he was, where he lived, and that she was about to say, "Darling, even one night without you was too long. Please hold me and never let go."

Right.

Sadder, even after she'd made it clear she had no idea she'd find him at his own address, the hopeful idiocy hung on to him long enough to ask her in for coffee and cake. Hadn't she made it obvious enough the night before that she'd had what she needed from him and thanks, buh-bye?

No, he had to slobber after a few more precious minutes of her time, to hear her voice, see her smile, stare into her eyes and realize what a complete sap he was.

If he needed further proof of her lack of interest than her rejection of his coffee, her notable absence at the house today was it. By being gone all day she'd avoided even having to walk past him among the other workers. So. Enough. Time to put Darcy to bed, figuratively speaking.

Seeing her this morning cleared up the final mystery of why he felt so strongly that he knew her, which he'd been all too ridiculously willing to chalk up to some nutball theory of subconscious love connection. Of course he thought he knew her. He did, though he could barely extract her from his memories. Another of the neighborhood girls hanging around, giggling and preening, hoping for a glimpse of Cam. His cousin Bruce had married her best friend Molly, whom Tyler remembered more vividly than Darcy for the somewhat embarrassing reason that Molly had been one of those girls who, er, matured early.

Teenage boys were so deep.

So much for love at first sight, little sister Katie. Or second sight. And it looked like he wouldn't be given a third.

He parked his bike in its place next to the mower and slapped the garage door button as he stepped back onto the driveway, where he stretched carefully, not eager to start another day of painting sore and stiff.

That done, he let himself into the house, thinking a hot shower and a cold beer sounded better than just about anything—even another night with Darcy.

Okay. Forget that.

She was the first woman he'd been interested in since Annie had flattened him by refusing his marriage proposal. Obviously he was overromanticizing Darcy out of some vain hope he'd be able to avoid the scummy mess of the dating pool by falling back in love on his first try. Thank God she was blunt about her feelings—or lack thereof. He'd shower her off, too, then throw something together for dinner. Maybe a frittata— he had some leftover ratatouille that would be delicious in it, maybe with a few potato slices thrown in. Then he could sit back, relax and think about her. Or think about why he shouldn't think about her. Or think about not thinking about her.

He was screwed. And not the way he wanted to be.

The shower was refreshing, the beer cold and satisfying, the frittata slightly overcooked, but good anyway. He cleaned up the kitchen and took a second beer and his cordless phone out onto the back patio, where he'd optimistically set one of his cedar outdoor chairs, though he'd wait to bring the rest up from the basement. With weather this warm, it was tempting to haul out the grill and plant his vegetable garden, too, but Milwaukee undoubtedly had a week or two of chill still planned before it allowed summer to land for real.

He set his phone on the arm of the chair and laughed in disgust at his foolish optimism. *Hello, Tyler.* She didn't know the number. She wouldn't call. She didn't want to see him. Losing Annie must have made him cling like a burr to the first woman who caught his eye.

The phone rang. He blinked at it, adrenaline setting off a tornado in his stomach.

Darcy?

No, for God's sake. He took another swig of beer before he picked it up, imagining her voice on the other end even as he told himself not to bother.

"How are you, my man?"

Tyler smiled. See? Not her. And he was completely fine with that. Really. "Hey, Bruce, how goes it?"

"Not too bad. Just back from my workout and cracking open a brew."

"Back from your what?" He couldn't have heard right.

"I'm a changed man. Lost ten pounds this month and going for forty more."

"Forty! You're kidding. I've only seen you exercise your beer muscle."

"I know, I know." He laughed the big Bruce laugh everyone knew him by. "I met this woman. Whoa, you should see her. Personal trainer. She says no pain no gain. I'm telling you, looking at her I don't care what she makes me do. I feel no pain at all."

"Um…well." Tyler leaned back, slightly uncomfortable. Maybe when he was married he'd understand that the whole ogle-other-women thing was harmless, but this wasn't like Bruce at all and he felt immediate loyalty to Molly. "Wow."

"Get this. She's not only a knockout, she's got a degree in philosophy. Can you beat that? Brains, biceps and boobs. The holy trinity."

Tyler winced. "That's…great. So, uh, how's Molly doing?"

"Fine, fine. Same as usual. She's why I'm calling. She's got this friend, uh…Darcy."

Tyler narrowly avoided spilling beer down his shirt. He had no idea how to respond to that, so he said, "Ugnhya?"

"Yeah, uh, she and Darcy are really close. They tell each other pretty much...*everything*."

Tyler sat up, then stood. "Everything."

"Sorry, man. Look, I wouldn't have called, but Moll said—"

Molly's irritated voice interrupted him from the background. Tyler paced off the patio onto his yard and down to the back fence, then realized his back fence was also Darcy's and beat a hasty retreat around to the front, not sure whether he was flattered or furious. Darcy had told Molly about their night together? Already? Had she discussed the size of his dick, too? He hadn't thought he could feel stupider for thinking they'd shared something special, but apparently he could. He'd like to have a word or two with her about privacy and integrity and good taste.

"Okay, Moll, if you're so gung-ho worried about her and I'm doing it wrong, then *you* tell him." Bruce's booming voice came clearly over the line. Tyler rolled his eyes. Whatever Molly had to say about Darcy's version of their night together, he wasn't interested.

"Tyler, hi, it's Molly."

"Listen, what happened between Darcy and me is between Darcy and—"

"I know. It's really tacky of me, and if I wasn't so worried about her and sure she was about to make a big mistake, I'd stay way out of it, I promise."

Tyler closed his eyes. Darcy was nothing to him. More to the point, he was nothing to Darcy. He owed her nothing at all. Not one thing. And if she was in trouble in some way and needed help, well, that was just too bad for her. She had the chance to... She could have... She...

Damn.

"Okay, what's wrong?"

"She got this crazy idea after…" She cleared her throat. "After things went so, uh, *well* last night. With you."

He rolled his eyes. Great. He got a good review. Call the *New York Times* and put it on the front page. "Yeah?"

"So she wants to do it again."

Tyler stopped dead on the sidewalk in front of his house and realized he was staring at Annika, the cranky eighty-year-old woman who walked her Scottie—named Scotty—around the block four times a day every day at the exact same hours. If you made eye contact she'd haul you into conversation extremely tough to escape from. He whirled around and walked back down the driveway, still stunned by what Molly had said. Darcy wanted him again? "She has a damn strange way of showing it."

"No, not with you."

Tyler closed his eyes. God give him strength to face this humiliation. "Thanks."

"I mean, she does want to be with you but she doesn't think she does."

He lifted his face to the sky. "Molly, you want to start this one over?"

"Yes. Sorry. Here it is. She's coming off a rough few years and she has this crazy idea of fulfilling all her fantasies before she leaves town."

"Leaves?" He couldn't stop the thump in his chest. "You're still ahead of me. Where is she going?"

"She's moving. To Seattle. Then L.A. Then Miami. Then Boston."

"For her job?" He didn't even know where she worked. He knew next to nothing about her. Why did he care this much whether she stayed or went or whether he ever saw her again?

"For fun. She's always wanted to live in the four corners of the country."

"Okay…"

"So I'm worried about her."

"She strikes me as someone who can take care of herself." And how. He couldn't keep the bitterness out of his tone.

"She's planning to walk into a bar dressed in some complete slut outfit and seduce whatever guy she comes across. On Saturday."

Tyler actually flinched, the pain was that real and that immediate. "Why the hell are you telling me this?"

"Because I want you to stop her."

"Me? You're worried about her, you stop her. Jeez, Molly, this is really over the—"

"She wants you, Tyler. She's totally fighting how she feels about you."

His mouth dropped open. He became aware that he had turned around and was staring at Annika again, who had planted her white-haired, blue-running-suit-clad self firmly at the end of his driveway and was beckoning. He shook his head and pointed to the phone. "Could you repeat that please, Molly?"

"I think she's really into you."

He frowned. Annika beckoned harder. "You only *think?*"

"I know she is. And I'm scared she's doing this second seduction out of some stupid fear she'll fall in love with you and won't be able to get away like she's planned."

Tyler couldn't move. Fall in love? What the *hell?* Had Molly lost her mind? "Uh, can I talk to Bruce?"

"Why?"

"Just…can I, please?"

Molly sighed and said, "Okay," in a tone that told him she thought he was exactly as insane as he thought she was.

Bruce came on with a cheerful, "What's up?" Annika stopped beckoning and pointed frantically to something in his front yard. Tyler felt like roaring at her.

"Bruce, man, how much of this is your wife's matchmaking fantasy and how much of it is real? My balls are on the line here."

"She's known Darcy since sixth grade, Tyler. I've never heard her say this about her before. Not with that boyfriend in high school, not with the old-guy one after. Molly knows people. She can tell you who's calling just by the way the phone rings. She can tell when women are pregnant sometimes before they know. She knows when people are sick—she has that sense. So if she says Darcy's in love with you, then she is."

Tyler had to ward off the thrill his subconscious happily provided. He shook his head, unable to process any of this rationally. Annika immediately nodded hers and pointed again. Exasperated, Tyler began walking toward her as slowly as he could. "So why exactly is Molly telling me all this?"

"She wants you to intercept Darcy at this bar on Saturday, so she doesn't make some stupid mistake with the wrong guy when she really wants you."

"You're buying this?"

"I know, I know. But that's what she tells me, and I trust her judgment."

"Tyler!" Annika's wavery voice was indignant. Her faded blue eyes glared under bushy salt-and-pepper brows.

"Bruce, I'll call you back." He punched off the phone, grateful for the excuse to escape, but not about to let Annika think he enjoyed being interrupted. "What is so important that I had to interrupt my phone call, Annika?"

"That." She pointed to his hedge. "What about that?"

Tyler turned and looked. A hedge. A house. He took a few steps closer to Annika and looked again. Still the hedge and the house. Nothing more noteworthy than that. "What?"

"Your hedge needs trimming."

He worked his jaw. He really, really wanted to say several

phrases that had grown popular in the decades since Annika's childhood. "Okay, Annika. I'll get right on that."

"Good." She turned away and started her familiar uneven trudge down the block, followed equally slowly by the equally ancient Scotty, who had once responded to a friendly gesture by nearly biting off Tyler's fingers.

He barely kept himself from making a rude gesture after her. Instead he tried to think about how lonely she must be and how empty her life was if bitching about other people's hedges filled her day.

Then without trying at all, he thought about Darcy dressed in a tiny skirt and tight cropped top, smiling at some megahunk in a crowded bar. He imagined the guy getting half-hard looking at her incredible body and her open smile and thinking he was going to get lucky in a big way.

Tyler stopped that image cold. So? If that was what Darcy wanted to do, fine. If she wanted to run away from any possible feelings for Tyler, that was her choice. She was a big girl, not a teenager. He wasn't going to chase after her and become her caretaker on the basis of one night together.

The hunk in the bar reached around Darcy's waist and pulled her close, leering. His hand slipped down to cup her ass. He leaned in and tasted the soft skin of her neck.

Stop that.

Tyler didn't believe in love at first sight. Not for himself and not for anyone else, either. Nor did he believe that sex necessarily had to happen in the context of a relationship, committed or otherwise. Darcy had enjoyed herself. He'd enjoyed himself. Maybe they both wanted more, but for whatever reason that wasn't going to happen and he was fine with that.

The megahunk's hand on Darcy's ass slipped lower; his fingers curled under her skirt and started up her thigh…

Tyler whipped out the phone and dialed. "Bruce."

"Yeah, man."

"The bar Darcy's going to Saturday?"

"Yeah?"

Tyler ran his hand over his face, checking in with himself for another chance to be smart and stay sane and stay the hell out of it. To make sure he really wanted to do something this stupid and also completely nuts and also freaking insane.

Another flash—Darcy lying under Mr. Megahunk, her nails digging into his hugely muscled back.

Apparently he did.

"I need to know which bar and I need to know what time."

5

DARCY CAREFULLY ADDED another layer of mascara to her already thickly coated eyelashes and blinked experimentally. She'd rimmed her eyes in black, making them look large and glamorous. Her lids felt heavy and the spiky tips of her lashes poked into the skin under her eyebrows, leaving inky slivers that then needed cautious wiping off. This dressing-up stuff was not for sissies.

However. Ahem. She looked—pretty amazing. In fact, stepping back to get a better perspective in the full-length mirror behind her bedroom door, she'd say she looked incredible enough to be someone else entirely. Which was, of course, exactly the point of the evening.

Wow. She put her hands over her mouth, careful not to smudge her Certainly Red lipstick by Revlon, which was…well, certainly red, and then she giggled.

Inventory from the bottom up: black, open-toed, high-heeled pumps. Outrageous stockings she'd stumbled across in the hosiery section of a mall store—thigh-highs with sequined tops that looked like normal sheer stockings from the front, but should she turn around, the viewer would be treated to an open view with rows of metal hooks holding thin, black satin ribbon crisscrossing from ankle to upper thigh. Next, a mid-thigh miniskirt in black leather with a big easy-to-reach silver zipper in back, over black lace thong panties. Continuing up, part bra, part cropped top in black leather with matching big silver zipper between her breasts. Then a big smile, hair long and tousled, color high and eyes wide with excitement.

Not her average look.

There wasn't a man in the place who wouldn't react one way or another. Whatever else she was tonight, she wouldn't be invisible, the doting daughter battling grief, the caring girlfriend racking up hospital frequent visitor points, passing time instead of living it.

She was a wild female animal on the prowl, and there wasn't anyone who'd conclude anything else after even the barest glance.

Darcy shrugged off her father's from-the-grave disapproval. Tonight she wasn't Darcy. She was…Ginger.

Too *Gilligan's Island*. Tawny?

Too porn magazine. Brittany? Too cute. Jessie, Caitlinn, Angela…

Angel. Perfect. Angel in the devil's black leather. Last name…O'Doomy. An elegant Irish name, which was of course pronounced "Oh, do me."

She giggled again. God, this was thrilling. She hadn't felt this ramped up and huntress-confident since that day in high school when she'd blown Evan Jacobus's mind with the teeny-tiny outfit her father eventually confiscated.

Well. Wait, though. She'd been feeling pretty extraordinary when she eased off her bikini for Tyler, before she knew he was Tyler. But this felt different. There was something…natural and right about that encounter, something familiar and inevitable and safe. The anticipation had carried the same intensity but her plans for tonight added the element of danger and the thrill of the unknown—though with her cell phone programmed to call either Molly or 9-1-1 at the touch of a button, the danger wasn't all that real. And some deep instinct told her she'd be well and happily alive and laid by the end of the evening. Which made her preparation nothing but exciting.

She strolled out of her room, swinging her hips more than usual—and what was it about the simple fact of a different outfit that could so affect how she saw herself? On the way she grabbed a tiny black purse and slung it over her shoulder, boogied down the stairs and out the door into her bright yellow Volkswagen Beetle, out the driveway and off on her adventure, heart pounding, cracklingly alive, as if she could power a floodlight.

Ahead of her, a night she'd always remember. When she was ninety-five, surrounded by loved ones on her deathbed, having lived a long, healthy, loyal and for the most part staid life, she'd have these wild times to think back on and be able to end her days with a wicked smile on her wrinkled face.

Downtown she parked in a garage near Milwaukee Street, stepped out onto the concrete and was hit with an attack of nerves. Crap. She should have done a shot of something at home, vodka maybe, to bolster her courage. Or worn a jacket or shawl to cover up until she felt brave enough to bare all. Definitely first thing inside she'd order a double whatever and slam it home.

In the meantime, no matter what she felt like inside, no way was she chickening out and no way was she going to let anyone see anything but total Angel confidence. Three steps toward the garage entrance her heel wobbled and a brief sharp pain shot through her ankle, making her hop unattractively for a few steps.

Darn it.

Okay. Settle down. Think positive self-affirming thoughts. Think of…Tyler's face through the window after she'd stripped and turned to face him. Think of the incredible zinging chemistry bouncing back and forth between her eyes and his, the immediate rush of hormones, the powerful excitement of the connection and the depth of sweetness when they'd been together. She'd done that. She could do this and feel all that again.

Shoulders squared, she stuck out her boobs, sucked in her stomach and headed for the door of Starlight City, looking straight ahead, woman on a mission. No nervous blinking, no eye contact, no sending out anxious glances to pick up on people's reactions, bad or good. She tossed her hair and opened the door, strode in as if she owned the place.

The wall of noise nearly made her rear back from the crowd of young bodies in the red-walled open space. To the right the bar glowed bright white, then neon pink, green, then blue. Darcy caught her breath, momentarily disoriented, feeling out of place, conspicuous, overdone, an imposter. She scanned faces hoping for a glimpse of someone familiar, when it occurred to her that in her current getup she wouldn't be familiar back.

Total disconnect.

A tall, skinny guy with greasy hair gave her a leering once-over, the lights in the bar reflecting red off his silver pierced nose rings. "Hey, babe, c'n I pull that zipper?"

Darcy started, immediately wanting to cover herself. What had she done?

Then…she thought again of Tyler. His admiration, his easy charm, his acceptance of her boldness. Nothing shameful, not at all, but exciting, erotic, thrilling. She could do this, remember?

"Zipper's by permission only." A cold look, the ice princess cometh—but only for the men she chooses.

"How do I apply?"

"You don't." She tried to stalk off toward the bar but her purposeful stride was impossible in the crush. She dodged one couple, came up against a foursome, started to say "excuse me," then realized Angel would never even begin to think she was invading anyone's space since all space belonged to her. She'd just get where she needed to go and people better keep out of the way.

Straight through the foursome then, with Mona Lisa lips.

By some miracle she reached the bar and ordered a vodka gimlet. As soon as it arrived, she sent the icy burn where it needed to go, trying to get her bearings, trying to recapture completely her certainty that this was a good idea and that some things weren't better left to fantasy.

"Hi, there."

She turned around, pre-icing her eyes just in case—and encountered the hunk to end all hunks. Ho-ly mo-ly. Blond, square-jawed, tall, muscles popping out of his black T-shirt, humma humma.

"Well, hi." She smiled invitingly, her heart giving a weird wistful thump while her brain thought of Tyler—without her permission this time. "Nice night for a vodka buzz."

"You bet." He grinned, showing perfect teeth, and moved closer, bulging biceps announcing he could crush her like a bug should he choose to.

Ooooooh.

"I'm Alex."

"Angel."

He chuckled in that knowing guy way that was the slightest bit irritating. "I knew I was in heaven the minute I laid eyes on you."

She gazed archly, pouting her lips oh-so-sensually, wondering if lines like that ever made women laugh in his face, because she wanted to.

A bouncy pretty brunette appeared at his elbow and locked her hands as far as she could reach around Alex's massive arm. She then sent Darcy the kind of look women have undoubtedly sent women who looked like Darcy throughout history. Namely venomous. "We're going upstairs to dance. C'mon, Alex."

"I'll be there in a minute." He spoke curtly, predatory smile directed at his little Angel.

"We're going *now*." The brunette's warning tone made him turn; her eyes held his in a challenge.

Darcy moved pointedly away. Let them work it out. If he wanted Angel he'd come after her, but better to demur in the meantime. Besides, if she made it to Alex's bedroom and he made another comment about being sent to heaven by his Angel, she *would* laugh at him.

Two steps away, another guy approached with purpose, dark, with some Latin blood, full lips, long lashes, that tough, pretty look that undid her. Ho-ly double mo-ly. When did Darcy ever attract guys like this? Ne-*ver* immediately answered that question.

"Hey, chica. You here alone?"

"Yes." She glanced over at Alex, trailing behind the brunette toward the stairs to the dance floor. "You?"

"I am now. I'm Carlo."

"Angel." She sent him a sultry look from under her lashes, thinking that if he'd really shown up with a woman and just abandoned her, he was a very, very sexy jerk.

"Can I buy you a drink?" he asked her breasts, which weren't in any position to reply, but then she hadn't put them on display like that for her own enjoyment, had she?

"Vodka gimlet. Thanks."

"Be right back." He gave her a melting glance, which didn't melt her as much as he probably thought it did, but it wasn't half-bad.

After she followed the progress of his fine rear toward the bar, Angel made a point of looking around to see what other fish were inhabiting this particular sea. Darcy might cling to the first guy who wanted her, but Angel had the gift of choice and the power and daring to work the room to her advantage.

Ahhhh. Yes. To her vast pleasure, Angel intercepted the stares of several men, many of whom fit her definition of va-va-voom. Her first drink was already loosening her inhibitions and she smiled back more than once. *You, with the home-coming-king looks, I bless with a smile. You, with the serial killer tattoos on your face, I pass over and shatter your hopes. You, with the weightlifter's build and tough-guy bald dome, earring shining in one ear, I return your wink. You, with the lined face and hair dye, I spit on figuratively.*

"Here y'go, my Angel." Carlo presented her with a drink, clinked his glass to hers and bottomed-up an entire martini. Whoa. Carlo apparently liked to drink. "Nice place, huh? Good crowd, good music."

She nodded and took a gulp of her vodka, noticing the slur in his words for the first time. Hmm. Drunk men made lousy and clumsy lovers. She remembered that much from the one time in college. "This place suits me."

"Me, too. You come here often?"

She glanced at him, hoping for irony, found none. "Not that much, no. You?"

"Ya, pretty regular. I like it here. Fun times. Dancing's good, chicks are hot, you know?"

Yeah. She knew. Somehow it had been more fun and empowering looking at herself in the mirror, delighted with the change, than imagining him classifying her as a Hot Chick.

"So, Angel…" He sidled closer. "What d'you do for fun? And how often?"

Smarmy. No other word for it.

Darn again.

"For fun?" She sighed. Had Carlo been sober and charming and displayed any obvious intelligence, she could have said something outrageous, like tie men up and ravage them. But the fading excitement of his considerable beauty faded further when he gave a hacking cough that told of a nasty virus or extensive and prolonged cigarette use.

Blech. Ptooey.

"I party like I'm almost out of time, Carlo."

His eyes darkened. "Chica, you're talkin' my language."

"My dad hates it, though. He's a cop. He'd be furious if he knew I was here. Last weekend he nearly killed some guy I was trying to get to come home with me. I visited him in the hospital yesterday, though, and he's going to be okay."

"Aw, come on." He laughed, a nervous wheezing sound. "Be serious."

"Oh, I am." She watched his grin fade as she hoped it would.

"Yeah?"

"Oh, yeah. Completely." Angel opened her eyes a little too wide, stared a little too hard and lowered her voice to an edgy drone. "That's part of the excitement, all the danger, don't you think? If you're not living on the edge sometimes, why bother living at all?"

His face took on a slightly panicked look. "Yeah, sure. Uh, listen, chica. You know, I came here with friends, just saw one over there looking lost. I better go talk to him, see how he's doing, okay? You okay with that?"

"Sure. You have fun. Thanks for the drink."

She smiled as he left muttering and shaking his head, probably thanking God for an early warning that allowed his quick getaway.

Who was next? The night was young, the crowd thick. Ahhhh, the dark-haired hunk in the corner, giving her the "C'mere, baby" stare. How bad could he be?

Ten minutes later she had her answer. Bad. Could only talk about his job and his mother.

And the next one, the surfer-dude-looking guy who didn't seem to be in touch with a whole lot of reality and who questioned her about her music taste and then informed her she was wrong to like every single band and performer she mentioned.

Also bad.

Okay. New tactic. She'd go up to guys instead of waiting for them to signal their interest. She'd take control, be the huntress not the prey. Even smarter, maybe forego the megahunks who never had to bother developing personalities and try for a boy-next-door type instead.

Bingo. Guy in the corner with two friends already talking to girls, looking around somewhat uncomfortably. Batter up. She prowled toward him. Here comes the pitch…

Strike out. Angel made him so nervous he kept stuttering and finally spilled his drink on himself and walked away.

Darn.

Ditto with the next, a cute, curly-haired, boyish blond named Frank, who, instead of responding to her wildly sexy yet subdued attempts to draw him into conversation, kept laughing and saying, "Babe, you are *so* out of my league. I'm serious."

Okay. Now what?

And then she saw him. Slightly older than the rest, maybe late thirties. Sitting alone at the bar, nursing a beer, watching the crowd with detached amusement that looked knowing and intellectual and sexy.

That one.

Angel made her very hot way over to a spot next to him and ordered a third drink, glanced toward him, tossing her hair back, then did a fake double take. "Well, hi."

"Hello there." His voice was deep and resonant, eyes light brown and intelligent, nose straight, jaw strong, cute freckle high on one cheekbone. She also liked his hands, one of which kept his mug company, the other of which rested on his long jeans-clad thigh.

"I'm Angel. You having fun tonight?"

"I'm having more now."

She grinned. "Can I buy you a beer?"

"You can, yes, thank you."

Perfect. Perfect. His name was Jake, he was a graduate student at the Milwaukee School of Engineering, he liked kayaking, skiing, ethnic foods, Green Day, Linkin Park, *Harry Potter,* and he could tell great and funny stories about coming to Milwaukee as an East Coast transplant.

Did she mention perfect?

They talked for half an hour, easily, like old friends. He touched her arm several times; the eye contact was meaningful. A definite score.

But instead of getting more and more excited and worked up over the half hour, she started getting more and more anxious. She couldn't figure out why, but when she stared at his lips, in spite of the fact that they were masculine and sexy, she just couldn't imagine kissing them. And though she flirted and batted her eyes and let him examine her body when he thought she didn't notice, she was about as aroused as she was when she was talking to her cousin Joe.

What was the matter? Had she had too much to drink? Was she PMSing and not as excitable? Had she been ovulating with Tyler and therefore at a more sexual time in her cycle?

"So." He shot out his arm, checked his watch. "What do you say to a drink back at my place? I'm in a condo over the lake. Beautiful view, and what happens there between us is entirely up to you."

Ta-daaaaa. She'd done it. Angel had been a wild success. Fantasy number two was complete.

Except she didn't want to go.

Honestly. She was being silly; probably all the nerves had subdued her libido. All she needed to do was to go back to his condo and everything would fall into place. Plus, he'd given her an out in case she didn't want to go all the way, though really, what harm was there as long as they used condoms?

She smiled, ready to accept in spite of her misgivings, to

complete her adventure and have those stories to think about on her old-lady deathbed, when she was jostled from behind. She turned to scowl at whoever had invaded Angel's space, interrupting her fantasy-culminating moment, and found she was entirely unable to scowl.

"Tyler?"

"Darcy." He looked as astounded as she felt. "I can't believe it. What a coincidence."

"Um. Yeah. Yeah." She looked back at Jake and shifted her body to include Tyler in a strained social triangle. She'd introduce them and then she and Jake could…what? Leave together? In front of Tyler?

Oh, Lord. "Jake, this is Tyler. A friend. Uh. He knows me as Darcy. Which is why he called me…Darcy."

"Hey, how are you? Nice to meet you." Tyler extended his hand and the two men shook. Then Tyler put his arm down on the bar behind her and his fingers brushed over her back on the way.

Boom. Her libido went into overdrive. She wanted to turn around, grab him, clear the bar and make him take her right here, right now, in front of everyone.

So much for not-the-right-time-in-her-cycle.

She smiled nervously at Jake, who was chatting pleasantly with Tyler, being the all-around polite and nice person he was. Darcy turned to pick up her drink, and as she did she moved slightly so her shoulder dipped in toward Tyler's chest and his arm touched her back.

Boom. Again. More. Oh, my God.

She shifted toward Jake, gulped her drink and put a frozen smile on her face.

"What do you think, Darcy?" Tyler had said something and was now looking at her expectantly.

She looked back, wondering if she could fake having listened or if…if…

Oh. My. She now understood the expression "drown in someone's eyes," because his were blue-green and intent on hers and she could barely get her breath, let alone form a coherent sentence. She wanted to go on and on staring.

No, she didn't. She wanted to get naked and she wanted Tyler naked and she wanted it now.

And then there was Jake.

"Actually, Angel and I were about to get going. Back to my place." Jake put his hand possessively on Darcy's arm. She wanted to shake it off. What had come over her? Poor Jake. Nice, nice guy.

Yawn.

"Oh." Tyler didn't take his eyes off Darcy's. "Is that right?"

"I—" she took a deep breath, her shoulders rising up next to her ears "—don't think so. No."

Tyler's blue-green eyes got blue-greener—she swore they did—and even more powerful, so that she was drowning more deeply even than before.

Help.

She blew out the breath and turned to Jake. "I really enjoyed talking to you, Jake. It was a real pleasure."

And even then he was the perfect gentleman, nodded calmly, though he did flash a glance at Tyler that wasn't terribly warm, gave her his number in case she changed her mind, kissed her on the cheek and left the bar.

And. So. Here she was. Hot for Tyler. Again. Still.

"You look…" his eyes did a slow up and down, lingering on the zipper between her breasts, which made her skin come alive and beg to be touched "…amazing, 'Angel.'"

"Angel. Right. Well, I didn't want to pass around my real name looking like this."

"No?" He moved closer so she had to look up to meet his eyes, and the nearness of his body made her think about what it looked like naked, which happened to be extremely nice and very sexy. "What made you come here dressed like that? Do you do this often?"

"Oh, no. No." She laughed nervously, wondering why she'd rushed to deny it. Who cared if he thought she was a man-eater?

Obviously she did.

"This was just a crazy idea I had."

"Are you having fun?"

"It's been…interesting."

"Trying to get a guy to go home with you?" He pushed bangs off her forehead, let his finger trail down her cheek, leaving a path of tingling skin and a desire to be touched a whole lot more.

"I… Well, yes…" She didn't sound like Angel anymore, confident and sexual. She sounded sort of apologetic. Why should she be?

"So I guess I interrupted the big score with that guy, huh?"

She couldn't look away from his eyes. They were setting her on fire, she was pretty sure. Someone should check for smoke. "I didn't mind."

"No?" He moved closer, rested a hand on her hip.

She swallowed. Maybe they should get out of here before she set off the sprinkler system. "I don't think I was going to go with him anyway. Nice guy, but he didn't really do it for me."

"Ah." He pulled her toward him just for a brief second until their bodies made contact, then he pulled away. She nearly fell on the floor. Why didn't any of the other men affect her like this? Not even close. Not even close to close to close. "You want me to get out of your way, Angel, so you can try again with some other—"

"No." Her voice came out urgent and loud.

"Why not?"

"Because I want you."

His slow wicked smile made the color rush into her cheeks. "That's good."

"Why?"

"Come on." He took her hand and pulled her toward the exit. "I'll show you."

She followed. She didn't care where. He could take her to the most dangerous part of town and they could dodge bullets together, that would be fine.

Oh my. Angel must have had more vodka than she thought. She felt giddy and light and dizzy, only not the sick kind of dizzy, the fun kind. His hand was warm and he was strong and careful about leading her through the crowd so she didn't get bumped or pushed or stepped on.

Outside he hustled her along the street in the chilly air until they got to the parking garage where she'd parked her Beetle. She'd expected to be returning to it with some hot stranger in tow. Or not returning to it until morning.

This was better. Much better. And really, if she thought about it, being with Tyler tonight counted as her fantasy fulfilled. Because she'd dressed in the outrageous outfit and she'd gone to the bar, and look here, she'd picked up a guy.

Right? Now they could have the awesome sex she knew she'd get tonight, and then she could tick this fantasy off her list. Tick. Done.

He pulled her to the elevator, which opened magically as they reached the door as if it were waiting for their arrival. A middle-aged couple stepped out and Tyler very politely gestured Darcy in ahead of him. While they waited calmly, the doors closed, then they sprang together as if they were lovers lost to each other for weeks and weeks and now found again.

Or two people extremely horny for each other.

At any rate, in very little time Darcy found herself with her back up against the elevator wall and one of her legs lifted and wrapped around his waist. Their mouths hadn't been apart for more than a fraction of a second and their hands were exploring more territory than Lewis and Clark ever dreamed of.

Except then the elevator dinged and they pulled themselves together, smirking at the abrupt transition from crazed sex monsters to innocent elevator riders. Another middle-aged couple was waiting to get on, so it was just as well they'd contained themselves.

"Wait." Darcy stopped in confusion at the large number painted on the concrete wall. "This isn't the floor I parked on."

"It's the floor I parked on." He headed straight for a green boxy minivan, not the kind of car her Perfect Stud would be driving, but with the mood she was in right now, it was also the sexiest car she'd ever seen.

And it got a whole lot sexier when he pushed the unlock button, and instead of opening the driver's door, he opened the back.

He couldn't wait.

Her libido shot into higher gear than this car could ever manage. He held out a hand and she climbed in after him, giggling as he slammed the door and settled himself on the long seat.

"All aboard."

"Aye, Captain." She straddled him, hiking her stiff leather skirt up nearly to her waist to get her legs wide enough.

"Oh, man, Darcy." His hand explored the glittering tops of her stockings and up to the naked expanse of her rear around the thong. "Oh, man. If you had any questions about why I couldn't wait until we got home, just look at yourself and they're all answered."

"I didn't want to wait, either."

His strong arms came around her and he kissed her, and oh, she loved kissing him. They fit together so well, no loose lips or spit where it wasn't wanted. He kissed with perfect control and she was pretty sure she could go on kissing him for the rest of her life and be thrilled every time.

Hyperbole of course.

Eventually, though, her breath became short and her involuntary moans more frequent, and kissing was no longer enough. The hot bulge in his pants lay right under the tiny cotton strip of her thong and the warm pressure was driving her completely insane.

She broke away from him, her hair a mess all over her head and face, and yanked the zipper down on her top so her braless breasts could spring free of the leather. In seconds he had taken one into his mouth, manipulating her nipple with his tongue and the other with his fingers. She cried out and ground her pelvis into his, feeling like a tame animal reverting to wildness.

He murmured her name, lifted her and fumbled with his belt. She slid off and helped free his erection, thick, hard, soft and so beautiful she was starved for it. Into her mouth, where she sucked ravenously, loving the sharp intake of his breath, the way his hands tangled in her already tangled hair, how he moved his hips, careful not to push too far into her mouth. Everything about him turned her on. Maybe it was just that Angel was a sex machine, but it felt like more.

"Tyler..." She got up to pull down her thong, bonked her head on the ceiling and rebounded against the seat, panting and giggling.

"Ye-e-es?"

She put her hand to his chest. "I want you in me."

"I want that, too," he whispered, and he brought out a condom from his pocket just as she'd started to reach for the ones in her purse. Instead she unzipped her skirt and managed to get out of it, staggering and nearly falling and laughing again, wild sexual adventures in the plebeian darkness of a minivan parked in a garage. Even the windows were steaming up with their shameful secret.

She hadn't had this much fun in forever.

And there he sat, condom on his straining erection, smiling

tenderly at her. Wait, tenderly? Trick of the light, must be. He opened his arms wide, welcoming her on. Her giggles stopped; she moved forward and straddled him on her knees, aching to have that magnificent cock inside her. Aching more to be close to him again. She lowered herself slowly, blissfully, loving that they made identical breathy moans of pleasure.

These fantasies beat the hell out of her past reality.

Except then she made a huge mistake. She looked at him again. And found he was looking at her as if he'd just seen some magical beautiful vision that was all he'd ever need for the rest of his life to be happy, and she felt an answering tug inside her, and that's when she decided they had to screw like wild bunnies or she was toast.

Fantasy fantasy fantasy.

She jammed her eyes shut and moved up and down. He gripped her hips and helped her along, planting long, slow kisses on her neck.

She loved long, slow kisses on her neck. How did he know? "Mmm, so good."

"Yes-s-s." He gripped her harder, tilted his pelvis, and suddenly her arousal was so intense and hot she gasped with it.

"Oh, my—oh." She made funny, breathy whimpering noises and the world seemed to blur. "What are you doing to me?"

"Shh, G-spot. Ride it. Go with it."

"It's—oh." She moaned too loudly; she couldn't help it. She sounded like a porn star except everything about her noises was genuine and totally involuntary. The heat built; she was dizzy again and soaring through a sexual haze where nothing was real except this man and what he was doing to her. The climax rushed at her through the fog; she grabbed his shoulders and hung on for dear life, nearly shouting as he pumped her.

Then ecstasy hit and she could barely stand the intensity, feeling as if her body were trying to turn inside out. And in the midst of this absolute bliss it struck her that she couldn't picture having an experience like this with a single guy she'd spoken to, smiled at, looked at or imagined in that bar tonight.

Oh, dear.

She came down, a sweaty, satisfied mess inside this amazing man's embrace and inside his car.

Best of all, he hadn't come yet, which meant there was more fun ahead.

"Lie down." His voice was terse, a bit hoarse, and she knew he was crazy turned-on by her coming, and that got her heated up all over again.

She slid off him and lay on the seat with her head bent up toward the window. Not so supremely comfortable, but this wasn't all about comfort. Somehow with more giggling from her and some remarkably adroit maneuvering from him, he positioned himself so he could slide inside her again. And instead of fading while she wished he'd hurry up, her desire rose and rose, and she welcomed him, urged him on, countering his thrusts, wanting it hard and merciless, aware they were rocking the van and hoping no one was passing by.

Then his pace picked up; she opened her eyes and saw him devouring her with his deep ones, and she forgot about the van and only thought about what their bodies were doing to each other. In the dim light his face looked male and strong, his hair fell in sexy tousled waves down his forehead, his mouth was a line of determination while his eyes closed now and then to give in to the sensations. Then his lips parted; he lifted his head, breathed in through his teeth, and his eyes returned to hers for his climax as he whispered her name.

Oh, my. She was caught, utterly, by this man. Like a fish on a hook, like a bunny in a snare, bear in a trap…

The last thing she wanted right before she made a clean break from her old life and her old familiar town was to get tied down again. She should go home now, get in her VW and make a clean break from him, too, while she still could.

He let himself drop gently, keeping most of his weight off her.

"Darcy."

"Mmm."

"That was—" He turned his head, looking puzzled. "What's that noise?"

She tuned her ear to outside the van and heard it. "It sounds like…cheering."

"Uh-oh." He lifted himself on his strong arms and peered out the window above her head. Then climbed stiffly into the front, turned his keys in the ignition and rolled down the window.

Shouts from outside.

"Way to go, dude!"

"Rock that Dodge, bay-*bee*."

Whistles. More cheers.

"You the man!"

Tyler waved, closed the window, took the keys out of the ignition and crawled back into the seat next to Darcy, where she sat frozen in horror.

"Apparently we had an audience."

"Oh, my God."

He grinned. "I'm thinking you won't want to get out of the car to get over to yours right now."

She shook her head. Help. No. She couldn't. He'd have to take her home. But that was fine; a little longer in the car wouldn't make a difference. She'd made up her mind and she'd be able to say good-night and goodbye then, same as now.

"Get dressed. I'll drive us home." He held out a hand and helped her to sit. "But there's one condition."

She rubbed the back of her neck, which had gotten a little banged up against a cup holder. "What's that?"

"This car only makes one stop."

"What do you mean?"

He stroked her hair, tilted her chin, leaned in and spoke against her lips. "Either you're spending the night at my place, or I'm spending it at yours. Because I have quite a few more things I want to do to you and there's no way I'm letting you go before I get to the end of the list."

She sucked in her breath sharply. She should say no, insist she'd walk home from his house or insist he drop her at her driveway.

But the thought of what he might have in mind and the earnestness of his eyes on hers and the gentle touch of his finger under her chin were telling her in no uncertain terms that she wanted to be with him a whole lot more than she didn't.

And maybe that was all she needed to know. Just for her fantasy tonight.

6

DARCY WOKE to the smell of coffee and chop-chop-clunk-tap kitchen sounds from downstairs. She couldn't believe she'd slept so soundly in Tyler's bed that she hadn't even wakened when he got up and left.

Mmm, ahhh, oooh, a big yawn and stretch and awareness of that blissful soreness from having been, oh, shall we say, active last night.

The man was gifted.

Another clank downstairs and a sizzle. Uh-oh. He was making breakfast for her. Waking up together, okay. Having breakfast together…a little too relationship-like for a fantasy. Her plan had been to wake up first, smile fondly at a sleeping Tyler, gather her clothes, which were probably strewn in a path from his back door like Hansel and Gretel breadcrumbs to mark the way, and leave. That was how one-night fantasies were supposed to end.

So far she'd blown it. Hadn't she?

So, okay, breakfast. Because if he'd gone to all that trouble—and anything that required actual chopping defined trouble in her cooking book—then slipping out would be terribly thoughtless. And really, how blissful to have breakfast made for her for a change. Her father had been an even worse cook than she was, and she had no idea if Greg could cook or not because he'd always expected her to do it. Like a good dutiful girlfriend, she had.

Fine, then. She'd eat whatever he'd made, which was starting to smell absolutely incredible, and then she'd say, "Tyler, thanks for being my perfect fantasy last night. See ya."

Okay? Okay.

She got up, thinking fairly wistfully that it would be fun to go downstairs wearing exactly what she was wearing now, namely nothing, to see if his appetite for breakfast turned into a hunger for something else. But she was sore and, well, after last night, enough should be enough, shouldn't it? Though she didn't feel she'd had remotely enough of Tyler yet.

Danger, danger. Darcy-and-Tyler was over now. It should have been over after the window-undressing, but last night seemed to have worked out, ohh, pretty well.

Therefore she wouldn't go downstairs naked, nor would she put Angel's outrageous outfit back on. She'd borrow one of his shirts and a pair of shorts or boxers and go down looking scruffy, and that would be that.

Except when she walked into the kitchen, carrying Angel's clothes, which she'd found in various odd places, wearing a pair of blue boxers and one of his T-shirts, Tyler looked her up and down in a way that suggested he found the outfit even sexier than Angel's outrageous getup. In fact, the front of his shorts expanded in a way she found extremely inviting, though she tried not to let on that she noticed or that she was drooling over the sight, figuratively speaking.

"Good morning." His smile was soft and affectionate, and little thrills ran up and down her body as if it had been invaded by ants. Only it felt much nicer than that sounded.

"Hi." She tried to keep her voice flat and her lips in a straight line, but they wanted desperately to answer his smile, so she had to let them.

"Sleep well?"

"Yes. Very." And now she had to escape his gaze, which was

unleashing more and more ants the longer he trained it on her, or she'd start falling apart. So she stood next to him at the stove to watch him cooking what looked like onions and green peppers and slices of jalapeños. Mmm.

Unfortunately, being this close to him made her want to touch him, and obviously it had the same effect on him, because he put down his mug of coffee and put his arm around her waist, and then what could she do but rest her hand on his shoulder and move in close? She didn't want to be rude. Of course.

"That smells wonderful."

"Thanks. Mexican omelet sound good?"

"Perfect." Whatever that was, she wanted it. She was ravenously hungry. And now that his hand had left her waist and was curving gently over her rear, she was...ravenously hungry. "Coffee?"

"Sorry, over there." He pointed with his spatula and took his hand away, which was what she'd wanted, but now that he'd taken it away, where was the fun in that?

She poured herself coffee and seated herself at the kitchen table, already set for two, which should be setting off many urgent messages that she needed to leave *soon*.

"Mmm, good coffee."

"Thanks." He threw her a smile, but this one was a little distracted. "So, what's this I hear about you leaving town?"

"Oh, yes!" Her heart gave a funny painful throb instead of its usual badaboom tattoo of excitement. "I'm leaving on June fourth, my dad's birthday, three weeks and three days from now."

"Going to wander the continent?" He got a carton from the refrigerator and started cracking eggs into a bowl.

"When I was little I read a story about a boy who wanted to travel to the four corners of the earth. At the time I thought that was stupid because a circle doesn't have corners. But the U.S.

is sort of a rectangle, so I decided back then that I'd travel to the four corners of the country instead."

"And now you're going to."

"I've lived here all my life and spent a lot of years caring for my dad and then this last year caring for…a sick friend." She stared down into her coffee, not sure why she felt odd telling Tyler about Greg. "So I haven't been free to go anywhere until now."

"Sounds like the perfect escape."

She looked up from her cup. "Escape makes it sound like my real life is here and I'm running away. It's more that I've been kept here by circumstance, and now I'm finally able to start my real life."

"Okay." He beat the eggs in a bowl and she wasn't sure what he was thinking with a noncommittal response like "Okay."

But then his approval shouldn't matter to her one way or another. Should it?

"So I'm going to Seattle first, then Los Angeles, then Miami, then Boston. Two years in each place."

"That's a long time to be away." He poured the eggs into the pan and stirred expertly.

Darcy frowned. He still hadn't understood. "I won't be away. I'll be gone."

"Meaning…"

"I'm not necessarily coming back."

"Really?" He shook the pan, stirred some more.

She couldn't tell what he was thinking when he said "really" any more than she'd been able to when he said "okay," so she was going to drop the whole thing.

"You're teaching in the fall. Did you always want to be a teacher?"

"No." He sprinkled a big handful of cheese onto the omelet, turned off the heat. "I wanted to be a cyclist and ride for the U.S."

"Wow. That's so cool." She looked at his solid muscled body, thought of him pedaling around the Alps in the Tour de France wearing one of those skintight outfits, and got rather warm. Or maybe that was the coffee. "Why didn't you pursue that?"

"My parents didn't approve. Then Cam died in a motorcyle accident." He put two pieces of toast in the toaster, then rolled the huge omelet onto a waiting plate and brought it to the table. "The same year a kid in my class was killed by a car while he was riding his bike. I couldn't do that to Mom and Dad."

"Oh, my God." She stared helplessly while he divided the omelet onto two plates, then got jars of salsa, and tubs of sour cream and guacamole from the refrigerator. "So you gave up your dream."

He shrugged and put a plate in front of her. The aroma made her stomach sit up and beg. "I suspect deep down I probably knew I didn't have what it took. After Cam died I did everything I could to become the perfect child so my parents wouldn't have to worry about me like they did about him."

His story hit home. She knew exactly what he'd felt. "Perfection is a pretty nasty burden for a kid."

He looked surprised, as if he hadn't expected her to understand, and their eyes met for the first time in a deep connection that had nothing to do with sex. "Yes."

"My mom died when I was twelve. I remember feeling it was my job to cheer Dad up and become the woman of the house. He relied on me for a lot. And he traveled a good deal for his job, so I learned to cope on my own."

"That's a burden for a kid, too."

She touched his arm, wanted to leave her hand there and hated that she shouldn't. "That's why I knew what you were talking about. And that's why my trip is the chance to find out who I am when I'm not being the perfect child and not being the perfect caretaker."

"Your dad was sick for a long time?"

"Years. Though he was in remission for a while in between, thank God. That was a really special time."

All Tyler did was nod and collect the popped toast, but she knew without him saying that he was deeply touched by her story, too. "And your...friend?"

She heaped salsa, sour cream *and* guacamole on her omelet while she decided how much she wanted him to know about this private part of her life. And then it seemed silly not to tell. "My ex-boyfriend. Greg. He was in an accident, got a serious head injury. No fun at all. Though it's amazing to watch the recovery. He was virtually helpless at first, then he slowly started to reclaim his motor skills and his personality. Fascinating if you could divorce your personal feelings from it."

"Which I'm sure you couldn't."

She carefully cut a bite of the omelet with her fork while she debated further how much to share. The more he knew, the more this became about friendship as well as sex. And friendship plus sex equaled Darcy's broken heart when she had to leave. Or rather wanted to leave.

"I...had actually broken up with him before the accident."

"But you stayed to help him?"

"For a year. Yes. I couldn't leave him then. It would have been..."

"Understandable."

"But not right." She accepted the toast he'd buttered for her, but turned away from the admiration in his eyes before it went to her head.

"A lot of time in hospitals for you. A lot of worrying. A lot of responsibility and sacrifice. Very tough, I'm sure."

She stopped with her first mouthwatering bite en route to her watering mouth. She hadn't ever felt she had a right to complain about how terrible it was for her. Every time she'd tried to say anything to Greg about the strain of caring for her beloved dad, all he said was, "Yeah, well it's no picnic for him, either," and then she'd feel horribly ashamed and guilty. "Yes. It was. Draining. Especially so many years in a row."

"Took over your life, huh?"

"That's why this trip is my time to reclaim my life. And me."

"You deserve that, Darcy."

His warm, sympathetic eyes were more than she could stand on an empty stomach, so she shoved the bite in before tears could start forming, and her sadness was instantly transformed into bliss.

"Oh, my gosh, this is, mmm…" she swallowed "…incredible."

He grinned at her genuine awe at the taste and she was suddenly terribly and goo-ily happy to have made him feel so good and so— *Wait, what was she thinking?*

She wasn't supposed to be this relaxed and happy and comfortable with him. She should be calculating at what precise moment she could safely get away and return to thinking about fantasies she wanted to fulfill with other men in other places.

Better eat her omelet fast and be done with it.

Except it was sooo delicious she wanted it to last as long as possible, and then of course she had to have a second cup of coffee because she was too full and sleepy to move after eating so much. During that fairly long time they talked about their respective childhoods in Wauwatosa—which custard stand was better, Leon's or Robert's; how often they'd been to the state fair; how many cream puffs they'd eaten there; how many times they'd seen the Barnum & Bailey circus parade at the start of the performing season. Then on to people they both knew and their school experiences, high school and college, and how he had a serious girlfriend named Annie in college and graduate school. He went still and cautious when he talked about Annie, which meant he still had feelings for her, and therefore Darcy instantly hated her.

That intense response was her cue to get the heck out of here, *now*.

"Well." She stood and noticed his look of surprise at her abrupt move, then wanted to smack herself for being so unsubtle. "I should go. Thank you for breakfast. It was really wonderful. And for last night, which was…really wonderful."

"Right. Sure. You're welcome." He'd stood, too, and looked at her with a little perplexed line in between his eyebrows.

She owed him an explanation, but how could she say, "Sorry, I have to go because I'm in danger of wanting this to be more than it can be"?

Either he'd say, "What, are you kidding, you like me? Get real."

Or he'd say, "I want it to be more, too," and then she'd have to say, "Sorry, no can do."

Either one sucked.

"It was great meeting you." She edged out from behind the table and stuck out her hand, which he looked at incredulously, so she put it down. "I'm not very good at leaving one-night stands."

"This was our second."

"True, but if I said two-night stand, it would mean two nights in a row." She wrinkled her nose. "Okay, that was ridiculous."

"Two one-night stands doesn't sound like enough." He took a step toward her. "Darcy…"

Oh, no. Oh, no. She knew what was coming. She couldn't let him say it because then she'd have to reject him, and that cast their whole relationship—using the word in the literal sense—in a much more uncomfortable light than if she could just get out now. This way, if she bumped into him again, which she certainly might, since he was still painting her house, they could be cheerful and friendly and not saddled with the baggage of he-wants-more-and-she-doesn't.

"It was really fun." She moved forward, kissed his cheek,

smiled for too long into his beautiful somewhat bewildered blue-green eyes, and turned to go.

Then realized she was wearing his underwear.

"I, um." She turned back, loathing the botched exit, and swept her hand up and down to indicate his shirt and boxers. "I'll wash these and get them back to you."

"Okay." He followed the path of her hand appreciatively. "Come by anytime."

"Right." She made a mental note to drop his clothes off while he was busy at her house, and scooped up the armful of Angel's slutwear she'd left on top of the bookcase in his back hall. "Okay, bye."

"What about your car?" He'd stepped after her. "Do you want me to drive you to pick it up at the garage?"

Crap. The car.

"No." She turned back again. "Molly can drive me over, thanks. Bye!"

She hurried to his back door to find it was double-locked and she couldn't get it open.

Crap again.

Worse, then he was behind her reaching for the upper ledge of the little door for milk delivery that many houses around here still had, though most were sealed up now, and when he brought down the key his chest bumped her shoulders and he smelled really, really good. She wanted to lean back and have his hands roam all over her body and make her feel that wild-woman feeling again that she hadn't ever felt with anyone else. At least not yet.

Instead she excused herself and stood out of the way while he unlocked the door, then shot past him into the cool morning, and of course there was Annika walking her dog and there was Darcy busted in front of Tyler's house wearing his underwear early on a Sunday morning.

Crap a third time.

She sprinted for his backyard, hearing Annika shout something angrily and Tyler reply in an amused voice. She dumped Angel's clothes over the fence, climbed over herself and made it safely back into her house.

Whew.

Except her house didn't smell like coffee and omelet and man. And for a long time she stood, leaning against the closed front door in the house she grew up in and was soon leaving, wishing with all her heart that it did.

7

WHAP. TYLER'S GOLF BALL rose promisingly from the tee at Storm's Golf driving range and immediately curved sharply to the right. A classic slice. Probably his twentieth of the afternoon. The stocky middle-aged man to his left whistled silently, clearly impressed by Tyler's ineptitude.

Tyler wasn't a golfer. Maybe that was too obvious to bother saying. He didn't even see what anyone could enjoy about a sport that was virtually impossible. Give him baseball any day, basketball or soccer. But he came to this range in Brookfield every year on May 11, his late brother's birthday, and hit a bucket of balls in Cam's honor. Cam had loved golf. Been damn good at it, too, as he was good at everything he tried. Maybe coming to the range was an odd tribute, but Tyler enjoyed it.

He persisted anyway.

Whap. Fade shot. Still curving to the right, but not as far this time. Half the bucket left for Tyler to reflect on his brother's life and repeatedly humiliate himself.

Sometimes he wondered what would have happened if Cam were still alive. Would Tyler have pursued his youthful dream of being a world-class cyclist? Without Cam to impress, would he still have had the guts to try? Cam had dragged him along on several idiot-brained schemes and Tyler couldn't deny loving the rush—not only of facing danger, but of being part of a team with his brother and pushing himself to physical limits. He'd rather have landed in the hospital than stay home and look chicken.

But after Cam died trying to jump his motorcycle over the family van, Tyler stifled whatever wild genes he might have shared with his brother. No skydiving, no bungee jumping, no driving drunk, no extreme sports of any kind.

On top of that, along with the shock and grief, Tyler had felt keenly the passing of the torch to himself as the now eldest and only son. With the flashy high-maintenance member of the family gone, Tyler's desire grew to make his own way and his own success instead of being satisfied to stay in Cam's shadow, striving to emulate an idol he was nothing like. In an odd sense he'd been freed to continue to grow up as himself and to reach for his own goals. Not that he'd understood that psychology at the time. Back then he'd just wanted to take the pain out of his parents' eyes and make them proud again. Giving cycling the backseat to more serious academic pursuits had been part of that, he was sure.

Whap. Hook shot, curving dramatically to the left this time. Ahhh, something new. The guy next to him shook his bald head. Tyler looked wistfully at the bucket of balls, still half-full. He'd ten times rather be back in bed with Darcy, burrowed against her, burrowed inside her, laughing, talking, having orgasms that rocked the continent...

But even if he hadn't needed to ride to the range this morning, he wouldn't be with her now. Once again she'd put an end to their blissful togetherness way sooner and more abruptly than he'd wanted, though he found it interesting she'd rushed for the exit when he'd started talking about Annie.

Even if Darcy still suffered from jitters, Tyler was pretty sure he could convince her to go out with him again. And again after that and again and yet again. If she felt about him the way Molly and Bruce thought, feelings he glimpsed now and then when they were together—or thought he did—and if he continued to feel this strongly about her, who knew where they could go? Maybe all the way.

Whoosh. Missed the ball completely. Bald Guy snorted. Who liked this game? Why? Cam better appreciate this, wherever he was. Probably laughing his ass off at his lame brother.

Cam's lame brother had showed up last night at Starlight City shortly after ten, feeling like a creep stalking a woman who gave every sign of not wanting to be around him. It had taken Tyler a few minutes to find her in the crowd, and when he did, he'd nearly passed out. Had any woman ever looked that sexy? Ever? He'd had to work hard not to punch the muscled dork drooling all over her, and the dark-haired pretty boy after that, and the one after that and, oh yeah, the next one, too. She certainly knew how to work a room.

Somehow he'd stayed invisible, enjoying watching her try to pick up men about as much as breaking his wrist when he fell off Cam's handlebars.

Twice, when she'd given some guy a cock-stiffening, come-on-baby glance, he'd said to hell with it and stalked toward the exit. Twice he'd reached the door and hadn't been able to abandon her to the wolves. Or abandon the wolves to such an effective huntress. Especially when man after man apparently failed whatever test she was issuing. What was she really searching for?

Him?

Just when it started to look as if she'd reject every man she met and he could escape home unseen to report Mission Prevent Seduction a success to Molly and Bruce without having to lie to Darcy about why he'd ended up at the same bar the same night at the same time, Darcy had landed on that Jake guy and hadn't taken off again.

No matter how many times he told himself that what she did with her evening and her time and her body was none of his business, Tyler hadn't been able to sit back and watch her score. And not because Molly was worried. He'd had to talk to Darcy, touch her, make sure she remembered who he was. The way her eyes brightened when she saw him, the way she reacted to his casual touch, the way their vehicle-rocking lovemaking had been both wild and sweet…hope had risen in his chest and stayed there even now, even after she'd bolted from the breakfast table.

Though he didn't think he'd ever be able to drive his van again without getting a hard-on.

Whap. Pushed that one slightly to the right, a mere hundred and fifty yards off Cam's old driver. But, hey, an improvement, right? Bald Guy gave him a condescending thumbs-up and hit yet another perfect shot, straight and long.

Show-off.

Everything else about the day felt good. More than good. Colors seemed brighter, the breeze fresher, birdies tweeted more melodiously. Since meeting Darcy, Tyler felt he was coming alive for the first time since Cam died and took so much that was good from the Houstons' world with him. First time since Tyler had made that young and serious decision to survive and to thrive so no one in the family would ever have to suffer because of him the way they'd suffered because of Cam.

He stopped his swing. Wait. This couldn't be the first time he'd felt this way. The years with Annie had been thrilling, he was sure. He must have repressed those happy memories along with the pain she'd caused. Just when Tyler had been so sure the deal was sealed till death did them part, he found out Annie had stayed in touch with their Bowdoin classmate, the charismatic and arrogant Roger Jameson, who was also at USC then, and she did them part all by herself.

Whap. Damn. Back to the slices. If this was bread he'd have several loaves by now.

"Need a few pointers?" Bald Guy had hit all his balls and obviously couldn't take Tyler's amateur slashing anymore.

"I don't really—"

"Let your lower body come around later. You're hitting the ball with an open club face."

"Yeah, okay. Thanks." Open club face? Apparently that was bad.

He took his time balancing the ball on the tee, did a few practice swings, hoping the guy would leave. Tyler was here for Cam and his mind was on anything but golf.

Cam. Darcy… It had taken all his acting ability to react to her trip plans as though he thought they were a wonderful idea. Maybe he could persuade her not to leave town. Maybe he could get her to fall so madly in love with him she'd decide to stay in Milwaukee on her own. Of course he'd have to try. What choice did he have? He didn't feel as if he could do anything else but moon over her, scheme over how to see her next. A prisoner of his own foolish heart. Just like Katie claimed to have been when she met Edwin and Tyler had accused her of basing her life on a romantic fantasy. Yeah, well, guess what?

He aimed carefully, concentrated on his lower body and on the club face.

Whap. A pure shot, straight, long, a thing of absolute beauty. For all his disdain for the fussiness of the game, he couldn't help a thrill of pleasure. *That one's for you, Cam*. One out of a hundred, yeah, but at least he got one.

"There you go." Bald Guy did that really annoying gun thing with his fingers, then to Tyler's relief, he ambled slowly off the range, swinging his bucket, obviously pleased with himself.

At the end of his own bucket, Tyler would call Darcy and ask her out again. Suggest some casual fun since she appeared still to be feeling skittish. A trip to the zoo or a stroll along Riverwalk downtown to find somewhere for lunch…

Whap. Another one straight and true. *That one for Darcy. Whap*. A third. Just for himself. He was the *man. Whap. Whap. Whap.*

One ball from the end of the bucket his cell phone rang. Adrenaline surged. Darcy, beating him to the call? Change of heart? Couldn't wait to speak to him? He pulled his phone out and peered anxiously at the screen.

The number was immediately familiar. *Annie's* home number. What the hell?

"Is this Tyler?" The voice was loud, anxious, the words overenunciated. He smiled with affection. Annie's mom, who'd treated him like the son she'd never had. He hadn't spoken to her since he and Annie broke up. Now suddenly he missed her.

"Emily. What a nice surprise. How are you? How is everything?"

"Fine, dear. It's so good to hear your voice. Your mom said you just moved back to Wauwatosa."

"I'll be teaching at UWM in the fall."

"Wonderful! She and your dad must be so proud."

"I guess they are." He scratched the back of his neck, lifted the brim of his baseball cap and tapped it back down. Talking with Emily felt surreal, as if he'd been transported back in time.

"Annie is back in Milwaukee, also."

"Really." He started to sweat. Annie was back? She'd stayed in sunny California to be with Roger. A man she "loved the way she always suspected love could be." "Home for a visit?"

"No…" Her voice was cautious. "To stay."

"Ah." He took off his cap, really feeling the heat now, and fanned the brim in front of his face, picturing her soft brown eyes and sweet smile.

"Things with Roger…didn't work out."

His heart thumped in his chest. Annie was free. Annie was home. "I'm sorry to hear that."

"You are?"

"Uh…" How the hell was he supposed to answer that? "I…hoped she'd be happy."

"She wasn't. She's still not. She's been moping around here for a few weeks trying to figure out what's next for her."

He closed his eyes. Why now? Why not last week or the week before, or hell, any time in the past year except today? This was a moment he'd hoped for, dreamed of, prayed for fervently for months before he finally accepted that Annie was gone and could let her go. Almost. But he'd woken up with someone else this morning, and had every intention of pursuing a relationship with Darcy in spite of the fact that she didn't seem to want one and was leaving town.

Now Annie. Here. Unattached.

"I know she'd like to see you, Tyler. I want to invite you to dinner on Wednesday."

"Oh…thanks." He couldn't imagine it. Sitting across from the woman who'd smashed his heart, trying to eat and make polite conversation while her mother looked on? Um, no. "Actually, that's not a good night for—"

"How about Thursday? Or Friday?"

He put his cap back on. She'd keep at him until he either agreed to come to dinner or made it clear he'd rather chew glass. "Emily, I'm not sure it's a good idea. A lot of time has passed. I think we're better off—"

"Annie really wants to see you, Tyler. She knows she made a mistake and she'd like to find out…that is, she'd like to see…you."

Oh, boy. Even a few days ago he'd have jumped at the opportunity to try to patch things up with Annie. Or maybe not jumped. Stepped forward. Cautiously. But now…

"People deserve second chances, Tyler. You and she were so

good together. I know she hurt you, but she regrets it. It's crazy to throw away a chance for happiness out of pride."

Was it? Maybe it was. He didn't know, couldn't think objectively about anything that concerned Annie. Or Darcy.

"Would you mind if I took some time to think it over?"

"Of course not. But I hope you come. I'd love to see you, too, and Fred asks about you all the time."

"Give him my best." Tyler signed off and stared at the one lonely ball sitting in the bottom of the wire bucket, missing Annie as if she'd only left him yesterday.

In the next second, thoughts of Darcy superseded, stronger, fiery, exciting, and just as compelling.

He was going to lose his mind.

Last ball, teed up carefully, making him think about Cam, which made him think about how much Cam would have enjoyed being in this same position—intimacy possible with two women? Tyler was nearly overwhelmed just considering it.

Annie was back. A mighty swing and the ball curved sharply, cutting across the shots of several other golfers to his right.

Slice.

He picked up the bucket, hoisted his clubs and trudged back to the ball shack. In his car, instead of calling Darcy, he turned onto Highway 100 then left on Burleigh, right on Lisbon. So many restaurants and shops and businesses he'd visited here with Annie. The town was full of her, so many good memories, so many hopes for a long happy future. All gone. And now back?

At home, he pulled into the garage. He and Annie had planned to rent a place until they could buy this house from his great-aunt Marjory. Annie was fine returning to Milwaukee—Wauwatosa to be precise—with him, she said. Annie loved Wisconsin. Annie loved him.

And then she'd changed her mind about all three. Could he trust her again? Could he trust Darcy at all?

In the house, he shut the door behind him, stood in the back stairway and flipped his key ring over and over his finger. He could see the dishes he and Darcy had used that morning drying on the kitchen counter. Her presence lingered in this house, a place Annie hadn't been in since it belonged to him. Darcy's ghost would haunt him in his bed tonight.

He needed to hear her voice.

He dialed, feeling as if he were in a dream and only half in control of his brain.

"Hi, Tyler." She sounded surprised. Hadn't she expected him to call? After what they shared last night? "What's up?"

"I'm back from playing dismal golf, where I mortified myself in front of many, many people."

She laughed. "Golf skill doesn't count as a measure of a man's worth."

"No? What does? Wealth? Power? Looks?"

"Oh ye of shallow faith. How about humor, intelligence, honesty, respect…and good stuff going on in the bedroom."

He grinned, emerging from his dream state into her reality. "Come to the zoo with me today."

"Oh. Wow. I… It's just that I have a lot to do today."

Her flat response sucked the joy out of his grin. "Tomorrow?"

"I don't think…"

"Right." He took off his cap and tossed it into the TV room, not caring where it landed. "What's the deal, Darcy?"

"I'm sorry." Her voice turned low and sincere. "I really don't mean to make you crazy. It's just a bad time for me to start a relationship."

"Is that really true or is it an excuse to let me down easy?"

"Really true. I think you're great, Tyler. You're funny, smart, honest, respectful…and *good stuff* going on in the bedroom."

He managed to chuckle even though his gut was tensed for the blow-off he knew was coming.

"It's just that the more we're together, the harder it will be for me to go."

"So don't go."

She laughed tightly. "I've wanted to do this since I was a girl."

"I understand." He closed his eyes.

"Really?"

"Really." And why did he have to be such a bleeping nice guy? Cam would have used every weapon he had to get her to stay. He should have lived just so Tyler could have taken lessons.

"You're so wonderful." She sounded near tears. "Thanks, Tyler."

"So how about we go to the zoo and I act like a jerk so you won't fall for me?"

Her laughter was worth it. He wanted to make her laugh like that every day for the rest of his life.

"Tempting, but I think maybe not." She started to say something else, then sighed. "Goodbye, Tyler. I really loved meeting you."

"Right. Bye." Tyler hung up the phone and glared at it as if he'd like to punch it in the dial tone.

Damn it. This was crazy. Going after Darcy would be a long up-and-downhill chase. He had zero tolerance for that kind of mind game, even if she was so conflicted she couldn't help it. Whether or not Bruce and Molly were right about her feelings for him, what difference did it make if she refused to let them out? What kind of suicidal idiot would rush into heavy pursuit of a woman he barely knew who ran hot and cold and was about to leave town? How much more of his heart could he risk on someone who didn't know her own mind? Even Cam wouldn't be crazy enough for that dare. Or maybe he would. But Tyler wasn't Cam.

Annie was here. A woman he fit with, a woman he knew and trusted. Okay, used to trust. But, with enough time and talk, could trust again. At least Annie wanted to see him, at least Annie wanted to find out what could happen between them. At least he knew his feelings for Annie were based on more than an explosion of chemistry that had somehow taken over his brain and common sense.

He turned off thoughts of his sister Katie, married for two years now, happily, she claimed, though she'd never admit otherwise after Tyler had made his feelings so clear regarding her odds of success. Maybe he'd better go to dinner with Annie and her parents and brave the awkwardness. Seeing Annie could bring his feelings for her and his certainty about their future roaring back to life. In which case if her mother was right and she wanted another chance, they could take it slowly and carefully.

Unless seeing Annie didn't bring the feelings roaring back. Then he was screwed. Because it meant he was in even more desperate trouble over Darcy than he thought.

8

TYLER STOOD on the familiar front steps of Annie's house on Raymir Circle, a quiet, middle-class Wauwatosa street not far from the Menomonee River. In his hand a bunch of red tulips, interspersed with fuzzy greens and baby's breath. He felt about the same way he did senior year in high school arriving at Mary Kate Dawson's house to pick her up for the prom. Out of his element. Nervous. Excited. Unwilling to dance.

He'd spent the day wandering his house, attempting to accomplish things and not succeeding. Eventually he'd given up and taken a bike ride on the Hank Aaron trail from Miller Park to the lakefront, which had calmed him down enough to shower and get to the florist and then here in relative sanity.

The house looked the same. Not that he'd really expected huge changes in a year, but so much else in his life was different it almost seemed as if the property should reflect that.

He'd met Annie their junior year at Bowdoin. Both from Wauwatosa—Tosa to the locals—they'd gone to different high schools and hadn't ever intersected here. But they started intersecting regularly after they sat together on the first day of a geology class they were both taking out of curiosity. For months they were just friends, then their relationship had blossomed into romance over the summer, and continued even after Annie graduated and started a Ph.D. program in political science at USC Santa Barbara while he finished his senior year of college.

When Tyler also got into USC, he decided he was serious enough about Annie to follow her there, and the rest was history.

Painful history. Which better not be destined to repeat itself.

He rang the doorbell, a solemn chimed tune that Annie's mom loved because it reminded her of the church bells near her childhood home in London.

Emily Phillips yanked open the door almost immediately, imposing as ever at nearly six feet, and unless it was his imagination, it seemed to Tyler that her face fell when she saw him. He was here on the right day, wasn't he? Friday? He was positive that's what they'd agreed on. He was maybe four minutes late, but how bad could that be? Had he changed in some horrifying way?

"Tyler!" She recovered and beckoned him into a bear hug. "How *absolutely* wonderful to see you. Wonderful. *Absolutely.* Just…wonderful."

…*absolutely?* He presented the flowers, surprised at her show of nerves. Emily was usually very calm and spoke sparely. But then the whole family would probably be on edge. Better hit the booze ASAP so they could all relax.

"Tulips, how lovely, how just…lovely they are. Thank you. Lovely."

Tyler nodded, glancing around surreptitiously to see if Annie was hovering close by, checking him out before she presented herself. Maybe that's what was making her mother babble?

He could see nothing. The interior of the house looked just as hodgepodge and carelessly welcoming as it always had.

"Well, come in, come in. I've been calling Annie all day, you know. All day. She's with friends. And I haven't reached her. Not once. Not at all."

He raised an eyebrow. "She's missing?"

"Oh, no. No. I'm sure not. I just wanted to make sure, you know, that she, uh…knew. Well, never mind."

His stomach lurched. "She doesn't know about tonight?"

"Oh, yes. Yes. She does. She does." Emily gestured him to the familiar salmon-colored chair by the fireplace. "She certainly does."

Okay. This was getting extremely weird. "Well. Good."

"Would you like a drink?"

"Please."

"The usual?"

"You bet." He grinned and her face relaxed enough to smile back in the way that always reminded him of Annie. Same almond eyes and curling mouth. Though Emily's hair had gone gray and her face had become lined, she was still beautiful. Like her daughter.

"I'll be right back. Oh, here's Fred." Emily hurried toward her much shorter husband and they exchanged brief whispers before Fred Phillips forced his frown into a smile and strode toward Tyler, hand outstretched, his hearty attitude adopted to conceal shyness.

"Hey there, Tyler. Damn good to see you. Damn good."

Tyler put out his hand and found himself pulled into a manly back-slapping hug, which touched him. Annie had broken up more than just her and Tyler's relationship. These wonderful people would have been his other parents.

"How's life treating you, Professor?" Fred chortled and rubbed his hands together.

"Life is good." Confusing as hell at the moment, however. "Looking forward to starting teaching in the fall. I'm doing some house-painting in the meantime."

"How are your parents?"

"Here we are." Emily came back into the room with a tray of Manhattans, a drink the Phillips family had introduced to Tyler and which he always shared with them. They toasted each other, then sat—Tyler comfortably, the Phillipses on the edges of their seats—while Tyler filled them in on his family and his last year in California when he'd been finishing his Ph.D. He didn't mention that it took him months longer to write his dissertation than it should have, or how much trouble he'd taken to make sure he never ran into Annie and Roger, newly in love while he could barely manage to shave every day. Some things were better left in the past.

Besides, thinking of heartbreak reminded him too much of the moping he'd done all this week. As much as he'd hated working at Darcy's house last Monday and Tuesday while she remained hidden inside or otherwise gone, he hated even more that he'd finished the job and therefore lost any connection to her at all.

The Phillipses' front doorbell rang. Bing bing-bing bonnng. Bing bing-bing bonnng.

Emily and Fred shot from their chairs, glanced at each other, and fled toward the front door. Tyler rose slowly. Was it *that* big a deal for him to be seeing Annie again? Or was it something else? She was pregnant? She'd come back drug-addicted? Brain-damaged in some way?

Her familiar musical voice greeted her parents and his heart thumped harder. *Annie.* He stepped closer, eager to see her. Her parents were talking in conspicuously soft voices. Something they didn't want him to hear.

"Tyler?" Her voice rose in disbelief. "No. Tell me you didn't."

Tyler stopped cold. And there it was, folks, the explanation for the Phillipses' strange behavior. Somehow they'd neglected to mention to their daughter that the man she'd dumped a year ago, the same day he'd expected to be announcing their engagement to the world, was invited that evening for dinner.

Sweet. Really. Just great.

"He's here *now?*" Annie's voice again, lower, showing panic. "But I look like hell."

Her mother murmured a few words, undoubtedly reassuring. Tyler's grin took him the final few steps into the front hall. She wanted to look nice for him. That was good.

And there she was, not looking anything like hell. Her dark bob was windblown, her eyes looked tired, she'd lost too much weight, but her cheeks were flushed, she held herself straight and...well, she was Annie.

"Hi." He found himself grinning harder as she turned and saw him.

"Tyler. I didn't—" She glanced at her mother, then turned back to him and let a smile overtake her. "It's good to see you."

"Same here." At least she wasn't going to make a scene. And she sounded sincere. He certainly was. He couldn't stop beaming like a fool just at the sight of her.

Her parents stepped away from the protective circle they'd formed around their daughter, and he found it easy to walk up, envelop her in his arms for the first time in a year, rest his cheek on her hair and inhale her scent. *Annie.* The woman he never used to be able to hug without thinking how she belonged in his arms, made for him, forever and ever.

He wasn't thinking that now.

Uh-oh.

He released her and they smiled at each other in confusion. Glanced away. Glanced back. Away. Back.

Her parents jumped in, ushered them into the living room for another round of Manhattans, then into the dining room for Mrs. Phillips' goulash, which had been Tyler's favorite.

Dinner was delicious...and tiring. Lots of forced jokes, lots of stress-inducing silences broken by determined chatter. Many glances stolen between Annie and Tyler, sizing each other up, checking for differences, searching for attitudes, like animals sniffing for cues to their reception. Many other glances from Mom and Dad Phillips, testing Annie's and Tyler's reactions to each other.

All in all exhausting. Tyler was beyond relieved when the last piece of Emily's superb strawberry-rhubarb pie had been eaten and washed down with excellent brandy, and Annie suggested a walk.

God, yes. Get him out of this house.

They escaped into the twilight and the rapidly cooling air, down the driveway past Annie's blue Prius, which he'd helped her pick out in California, and along Raymir Circle toward Glenway.

"I guess I was a surprise tonight, huh."

"Uh, yeah." She chuckled briefly. "Mom doesn't understand that we split. She thinks everyone falls in love once and that's that. You get married and live happily ever after. That's how it was for her and Dad."

"So your mother hasn't gotten over me, but you have."

She took his hand and he held it, happy in a quiet way at the familiar sensation. "Tyler, I know you didn't believe me, but we were over long before I started dating Roger."

"Ah, right. That's why I asked you to marry me. Because it was over." He couldn't keep the bitterness from his voice.

"Actually, I've thought about it a lot. I think you asked me to marry you because you could tell I was pulling away and you panicked."

He had to force his breathing to relax, keep his shoulders down. She thought he'd asked her to marry him because he was afraid of losing her? Uh, no. "What a romantic view."

"Think back, Tyler. Really think. That last year after you came to California, nothing was the same. We were going through the motions. We never got back in stride after that long-distance year when it was easy to be in love because we barely saw each other."

"Oh, you cynic." That hurt. He didn't want to think about them that way. Worse, when he did force himself to recollect scattered impressions of that year in California before she'd left him, her words rang a few reluctant bells. He also remembered feeling unpleasantly manic when he'd shopped for her ring. The uneasiness had bothered him then, but he'd written it off as normal jitters.

Maybe he'd shoved memories of their past away for reasons other than self-preservation. Maybe he hadn't wanted to look too closely.

"I'm sorry, Ty. Am I hurting you?"

"For a change."

"Ouch. Don't be bitter."

"Sorry." He dropped her hand, put his arm around her shoulders and hugged her briefly. "You're probably right about all of it. I'm a guy. I don't do that complicated psychology stuff. I just know what I feel in my pants."

She smacked his shoulder. "As if."

"Tell me more, Annie. I need to get this straight, and I'm not angry or stunned this time, so I can really hear you."

"Okay." Her voice was gentle and affectionate. It warmed him—but didn't stir him up. "That last year all the energy and excitement between us was gone. We did our own thing about ninety percent of the time. The only hours we spent together were in front of the TV or studying."

"I figured we were just drowning in work and needed all our energy for that. I figured after we graduated and moved back here, things would get better again."

"We were drowning, but I don't think we had any chance of resurfacing." She nudged his arm with her shoulder. "If we'd really been into each other, we would have found time. Made time. We would have dug passion and excitement out from between research trips to the library."

He put on a fake leer. "Or during research trips to the library."

She laughed. "Exactly. We were content with each other, period. That isn't really love."

"And torment is?"

"After Roger, I'm starting to wonder." She squeezed his hand. "I'm joking. No, torment isn't love. But our contentment was closer to boredom than satisfaction. And we both deserved more than someone easy to get along with. We never really lit each other on fire. Not even at the beginning."

"On fire? What, and risk burning up?" He immediately and unwillingly thought of the heat he and Darcy generated together. "You're sounding like my sister."

"Oh, God, don't tell me you still haven't patched things up with Katie."

He shrugged, not wanting to bring that up again. But Annie was right. There had been no fire between them, even at the beginning. Only a peaceful glow. They'd been friends for weeks before it even occurred to him to kiss her. And the next time he saw her he'd had to remind himself that she was more than a friend so he'd remember to kiss her again. After that…just hormones and habit?

How long before he wanted to kiss Darcy every time he saw her? Roughly no seconds.

"Katie's right, you know. Love at first sight does exist."

"Oh, come on." He instinctively rebelled, for reasons that probably didn't flatter him.

"It does."

"That's what you had with Roger? Look where that went."

"No. Not even close. He was a convenient way to leave what was wrong with us. He was also your complete opposite, and the opposite of someone wrong for you is usually equally wrong. I was too…I don't know, dazzled, I guess. It's embarrassing to admit."

"You don't have to be embarrassed around me." Though he couldn't imagine Annie being dazzled. She was always so levelheaded. Always so calm. Her moods were easy, light and predictable. So were his. Maybe because they did bore each other. "Then how do you know love at first sight exists?"

"Because one or two of my girlfriends experienced it. My mom and dad had it, too."

"How did they describe it?" He wasn't sure he wanted to know…because he was afraid he already did.

"Intense excitement, but different from being infatuated, which was all I had with Roger. My mom said it was as if she already knew Dad. As if she already loved him deeply even without knowing him yet. She said it was hard to explain, but that if you'd ever just lusted after someone, this would feel completely different, and that's how she knew."

That was it. Every inch of what he'd felt for Darcy when they met.

Great. Love at first sight, a rare and wonderful thing, and he had to feel it for a woman who wanted no part of it.

Annie looked up at him slyly. "Why do you want to know?"

"Just curious."

"You've met someone?"

He shrugged again.

"You have, haven't you?" Annie pulled around to peer into his face. "You have, ha! Okay, tell."

"She's…I don't know. She's very…I mean… Well, when I'm with her, I… The thing is…" He stopped. What was the point? Annie was laughing so hard he couldn't be heard anyway.

"I have *got* to meet this woman."

"Why?"

"Because, Tyler, dear, obviously you've fallen for her. Splat. You're gone."

He had no idea how to respond to that. *No way? Yes, obviously?* "It's complicated."

"Course of true love not running smooth, huh?"

"No." He walked farther, enjoying the touch of her hand, the touch of the breeze. It should have been him and Annie married here, taking a walk out of their own house after dinner alone together. And yet...no, it shouldn't. He could see that now. "It's too bad."

"What is?"

"That we were so good together in so many ways, but we couldn't quite get there."

"I know. It would have been wonderful. I'd love to have spent my life with you. If..."

"Same here. If..." But "if" hadn't happened. The Annie Chapter was really over. "I hope I always know you, Annie."

"You always will." She turned and hugged him tight, both arms around his waist, where they'd been so many times before, then pulled back and gave him her sternest look. "But right now I need you to do me one very important favor."

"What's that?"

"Promise me that whatever else you do..." she tapped a warning finger against his chest "...you don't let that woman get away from you."

9

HMPH. DARCY SCOWLED through the leaded glass of her living room window at the clouds hurrying across the sky, drizzle turning the air into a translucent solid gray. Wisconsin's fling with spring was over, temporarily at least. In the mid-fifties today, gloomy and damp, with June merely two weeks away.

Typical.

She stalked into the back bedroom, which had been a family room while she was growing up, complete with a tiny pool table, play kitchen set, dollhouse and a TV that Dad hadn't let her watch nearly as much as she'd wanted to. Now her steps echoed on the naked hardwood and bounced off the bare walls. She peered out the back window. *No, Darcy, the weather isn't different on this side of the house.*

Another trip, into the kitchen, a bit of a brood over the sink, and back into the living room.

Today was clearly not going to be her most productive.

Moods like this rarely visited her. She felt restless and scattered, not able to focus on any task, not even able to try.

Blech. Ptooey.

She wasn't exactly Florence Nightingale, but during her nursing tenures, she'd been mostly patient and mostly calm and mostly focused, even if it was only on constructing an elaborate fantasy life.

So maybe that was it. Sprung from her duties, she was

caught in limbo between the end of that life and the beginning of her next?

Or maybe she just missed Tyler.

Darcy snorted. Ridiculous. How could she? She barely knew the guy. She'd been with him twice, and yes, okay, those two times were…well, they were…oh, "extraordinary" came close, but, well, *really*. She barely knew him. And look, she had so much to look forward to, years and years in new and exciting cities: Pike Place Market and the Space Needle in Seattle, Hollywood and Beverly Hills in L.A., the Latin scene in Miami, Colonial history in Boston. Cities loaded with Tylers, cities in which she could pursue new fantasies anonymously and have adventures even more thrilling than rocking in a van with a man who turned her inside out with a glance.

Okay, probably not more thrilling than that. Maybe *as* thrilling, though? Maybe?

Aw, crap. She'd done right by cooling things off, but she hated this. What was he doing now? Did he have other women here? He didn't seem the type to have several going at once, not like his brother.

Was Tyler missing her, too?

Her heart melted at the thought of their mutual pining. Had she hurt him? She couldn't stand it. But better now than if they got any closer, felt any more for each other, and then she had to leave, causing much worse pain.

On the other hand, they could make full use of the time they had…

No. When she left, she wanted to leave Milwaukee behind completely, turn away and say goodbye, see ya, so long. She didn't want to leave any part of her here, especially not her heart.

Back into the family room, another look at the sky.

Yup. Still there.

She clenched her fists and let out a crescendoing groan of

frustration. Now what? The house was packed, organized and cleaned; her car had been checked wheel to hood and the oil and other necessary fluids changed. She'd already mapped out a route to Seattle, made reservations at the swanky Alexis Hotel for her arrival and had a lead on a few neighborhoods where she could look into subletting a condo or renting an apartment.

Maybe she should leave sooner? Except she loved the symbolism of a Dad's-birthday departure, and Molly was organizing a farewell party for her on June second which she had to stay for—wanted to stay for.

She could plan to fulfill another fantasy, maybe. That would give her something to do. She still wanted to go somewhere refined and proper like the art museum and find a private spot to bring herself to climax where anyone might wander by—of course in her fantasy it was a hot young guy who aided her in her orgasmic quest, but even without him, the danger of discovery would be exciting. And the view of Lake Michigan from the museum was gorgeous.

But none of that helped her now. Her grumpy mood didn't lend itself to that kind of adventure, so that was out today. If she called Molly one more time, Molly would probably block her number. Molly thought Darcy should quit whining and find out once and for all what was between Tyler and her. Darcy thought Molly should quit whining about Bruce and his personal trainer and find out once and for all that there was nothing going on as Darcy had reassured her only a thousand or so times. See how complicated love was? She should be thanking her lucky stars she was out of it.

Yeah. Thanks.

She wrinkled her nose and stopped herself from going into the kitchen for roughly the thirtieth time.

Maybe she should take a walk.

Outside, the wind gusted, blowing drizzle and fallen green

mini bouquets of maple keys and dried leaves left over from the previous fall. Darcy tipped her umbrella toward the wind's push, pulled her jacket closely around her and started north toward Clarke Street. Her favorite walk was a quick circle, just over a mile and a half around Roosevelt Elementary on 74th Street, where if she was lucky she could catch kids out playing in the playground, busily climbing and jumping and skipping and pummeling each other into the ground. Though probably not in this weather.

She was passing Center Street Park, admiring the newly leafing trees—and wasn't it nice to have them coming back— when she heard the whizz of a bicycle approaching. Slowing. Pulling up next to her. Stopping.

She turned anxiously. Carjackers she'd heard of—was there such a thing as a bikejacker?

Maybe. But this wasn't one of them. Hair dampened by the rain, blue-green eyes vivid, Tyler looked at her with an expression of such questioning tenderness that she felt as if she'd swell and burst.

Steady, now.

"Hi," he said, as if the word meant something much sweeter.

"Hi," she answered brilliantly.

"Taking a walk?"

"Taking a bike ride?"

He grinned. "I was restless. No painting today because of the rain and I couldn't stand sitting around the house."

"Me neither. I think the walls were closing in."

"They'll do that if you don't keep an eye on them." He gestured toward the road in front of her. "You headed anywhere in particular?"

"No. You?"

"No." He cleared his throat, adjusted his feet carefully on the pedals. "Would you like to go nowhere in particular together?"

Yes, yes, God yes. Anywhere. But no, she couldn't. Because…

Because she knew there was a really good reason not to, and never mind that his serious greenish eyes were making her unable to remember what that reason was. She couldn't even call Molly to find out. "Thanks, but I think I'll just keep going on my own."

"Okay. See ya." He pushed off abruptly, pedaled across the street, turned and gave one quick wave before he bent low over his handlebars and started down the block.

Darcy watched him go, feeling as if her heart was being sat on by Andre the Giant. How could she possibly have been affected so deeply by this man in such a short time? When she'd started dating Greg, she'd gone in almost reluctantly. He was too old for her, she'd thought. Nice guy, but fifteen years seemed an entire generation. Then he kept coming around and kept taking her out and kept treating her like the most wonderful and precious thing he'd ever come across. Who could resist that? So she'd given in, quite happily as she recalled, and they'd settled into a comfortable routine, which got so comfortable she'd started to doze through her life.

There was nothing comfortable about the way she felt toward Tyler. Especially now, watching him glide down the block, enjoying the view of his strong back and his strong legs and his strong butt. A woman could get very distracted from her righteous and moral path in life by that kind of a view. But she was just as infatuated with his strong brain and his gentle soul, if anyone wanted to know the truth, and that was far more dangerous.

Halfway down the block, Tyler came to a stop. Turned and caught her watching him, which left her totally busted because she'd just acted as if she was most anxious to keep walking on a blustery mess of a day when any sane person would stay inside.

He beckoned, then waited.

Now what? She stood, pushed by the wind wherever it chose

to blow her. The drizzle turned into a light rain that darted under her umbrella to dampen her legs, if not her spirits. He beckoned again, which put her squarely in a proverbial agony of indecision. She absolutely could not encourage him and then push him away again. It was one thing to be seduced Saturday at Starlight City under the influence of vodka when seduction had been the point of the evening and he knew it. Quite another to deliberately encourage him now.

But, God, how she wanted to encourage him. Deliberately.

She was still standing, staring like a complete fool, so God knew why he pushed his bike in a U-turn and started back toward her. Apparently he didn't mind that she was a complete fool. Maybe as long as she was a complete fool over him, it was okay in his book.

He approached, pedaling powerfully up the slight hill. Resistance was starting to seem futile.

"I have an idea." A drop of rain dripped off his bangs onto his forehead, and good thing he wiped it off, because she wanted nothing more than an excuse to touch him. "Let's go to the zoo. As friends. We'll hang out, talk, watch the animals, come back and go to separate houses. No romance, no kissing, no rocking the van. Just a good time. What do you say?"

Yes, yes, God, yes. And yet. She didn't think she could spend any time in his company without wanting to jump him. It would be an exercise in extreme titillation and even more extreme frustration.

But the alternative was staying home, still extremely titillated and frustrated but without him, without fun, without him. Did she mention without him?

"I haven't been to the zoo in a long, long time." Note how she skillfully avoided making a decision.

"I haven't, either. Come to my house. I'll change into dry clothes, get an umbrella, and we can go."

"Platonically?"

"One hundred percent."

That was okay, wasn't it? Darcy's heart lifted nearly into giddiness. Sure. Of course it was. No harm done by a friendly outing, right? Right.

"Okay." She smiled shyly at her buddy, ol' pal, brother kind of guy, Tyler Houston. "I'd love to."

By the time they got to the zoo, the temperature had dropped and the rain turned steady. A dismal day by any account. A day to be inside, reading, sipping hot tea, making love under mounds of blankets. Not a day for a young couple—er, a couple of *good friends*—to be splashing around the zoo gawking at animals. But here they were and she couldn't think of anywhere she'd rather be. Certainly no one she'd rather be with.

"Where to now?"

"I like the big cats." Correction, loved the big cats. Though the ape house was pretty great. Tanks of glassy-eyed fish and snakes in an immobile stupor she could do without.

In the nearly deserted cat house, they paid respects to a noble tiger whom they obviously bored, being mere fleas to his savage soul. Cheetahs lolled together in another enclosure, sleepy and cute, but a lion couple frisking like kittens took center stage and drew them in. They sat on a bench, shoulder to shoulder, watching the playful animals along with a mom and two kids, who eventually left when one child had a restroom crisis. Then it was just Darcy and Tyler alone in the building with the magnificent animals. The mama lion bit at the male lion's flank until he swatted her and jumped away. Hardly beaten, she jumped after him, somersaulted over and ended up on her back, submissive but with paws up and ready for another tangle.

Tyler took Darcy's hand. She looked down at their intertwined fingers, then up at him. "I thought you said no romance."

"Haven't you ever held hands with a friend?"

"No. You have?"

"Oh, sure. All the time."

"Uh-huh. Even male friends?"

"*Especially* them. Practically every day."

She couldn't help laughing. And because he'd been so funny, she decided that she wouldn't make a fuss. His hand felt very nice and solid, and connected them in a way she liked. A lot.

"Do you feel sorry for animals in the zoo?"

He thought about it for a while, his brow furrowed. "Yes and no. I hate to see them caged, but they get good nutrition, good care and live longer than animals in the wild. It's easier to swallow when they were born in captivity, because it's all they know."

She dipped her head toward the lions. "You don't think some wild part of them still longs to be roaming the African plains?"

"I have no idea. Should I ask them?"

"Nah. I don't want to bring up difficult issues." She watched enviously as the male nuzzled the female's neck, and felt the need to explain something he hadn't asked about. "There's certainly a wild part of me that wants to escape captivity, and that's why I'm so anxious to go on my adventure."

"What captivity?"

"Wisconsin. Who I've always been here. I feel like if I don't get out, I'll eventually get so used to being in a cage I won't mind it anymore. That horrifies me."

He sat quietly, absorbing this, she guessed, but she wished he'd say something. She was fully prepared to be told she was nuts. Plenty of other people already had, including her father when he was alive, and Greg when they were dating, and Molly all the time.

"What do you think you'll find that you can't get here?"

Her turn to think. "I'm not looking for something as much as I'm leaving something."

"Captivity."

"Everything I know. Everything I've always known. The

sameness of it all since I was a girl. Also the years I put my life on hold caring for other people. Maybe it sounds selfish, but I'd like to care for myself now."

"I don't think that sounds selfish, as long as you're sure you're doing the best thing for you."

Oh, sigh. Now he sounded just like her father and like Greg, who both made sure she knew how much more right they were about everything than she was. "You don't think it is?"

He shrugged. "What I think doesn't matter. It's not about me. Just what you think."

Her mouth dropped.

"Wow." The syllable came out before she realized she'd said it out loud.

"Wow?"

"You're nothing like my old boyfriend. Or my father, much as I adored him."

"I hope that's good."

"It is." She turned toward him and had to turn away because their faces were so close she couldn't think of anything but kissing him. "Trust me."

He pressed her hand briefly. "I do."

She bent her head. Two simple syllables and she was choked up like a bride hearing them at the altar. "Thank you."

"Look." He pointed.

She looked. The female lion had moved to the back of the sloping rock floor. The male stood by the glass enclosure, met Darcy's eyes with his majestic golden ones for a few heart-stopping seconds, then opened his mouth and roared. Roared again, his flanks heaving. The sound, even muted by the glass, was impressive. Darcy could just barely imagine its effect on a dark night in the Serengeti.

She was mesmerized. The female lion looked bored. Apparently the male was no longer impressive to her.

When Darcy first met Greg she'd loved his intelligence and decisiveness and the impression he gave of having everything in life all worked out at a time when she was helpless and hopeless and scared by the recurrence of her father's illness. So she'd fallen into the relationship and into some degree of feeling, half suspecting there was more to love, and half-afraid there wasn't.

By the time they'd broken up, his decisiveness seemed controlling, his confidence in his opinions, narrow-minded. Maybe the female lion had been thrilled at first by the mighty roar of her mate, but now she was thinking, "Yeah, yeah, king of hot air. How about helping clean the den?"

"What do your friends think of your adventure?"

"Molly thinks I'll realize what I'm giving up after I'm gone."

"Possibly. But that wouldn't be such a tragedy, would it?" He nudged her shoulder with his. "You can just come home again."

"True." She nudged him back and her lips smiled without her permission.

"I'll miss you, you know. Crazy, but there you are."

Ow. She'd miss him, too. How was that possible after such a short acquaintance? "You don't know me well enough to miss me."

"I know. It makes no sense at all. You're probably not even real. I'm probably dreaming this whole thing. I'll wake up tomorrow and find I'm back in California, I slept late, and I have a dissertation to defend in ten minutes without having studied."

She laughed, but her heart settled into a slow painful thump and she could feel her cheeks growing hot. She shouldn't have come. This was a mistake. She'd deluded herself, thinking that she could spend a casual day with someone like Tyler. She needed to get back on the fantasy bandwagon to keep life light and fun and in perspective for the next two weeks. Too much time in Tyler's company made her focus too much on him and how he made her feel. There were good times to be had all over the city. All over the country. Maybe all over the world.

Right. That sounded like a travel ad for a cheap hotel chain.

"I've blabbed enough. Tell me more about you, Tyler. Why did you come back to Milwaukee? Just for the job at UWM?"

"Mostly. I have family here, and my ex-girlfriend does, also. That's why I originally took the job."

She didn't want to hear about his girlfriend, which meant she needed to as soon as possible. "So you broke up with her recently? You were planning to move here together?"

"Bingo." He nodded, eyes on the lions. "I had dinner with her last Friday, as a matter of fact."

Darcy was very sure it was a good thing that she wasn't a malicious person because she'd be very tempted to track this woman down and threaten her with maiming if she came within ten feet of Tyler again.

"Really?" She kept her tone bland. "And how was that?"

"Emotional." His voice thickened.

Skip the threats. Proceed directly to maiming. "I can imagine."

He didn't have to know what she was imagining, however.

"Though by the end of the evening, I understood more about our relationship and why it didn't work. That put a lot of doubts and ghosts to rest. Finally."

"Oh. That's good." She exhaled her relief, managing to sound neutrally enthusiastic, instead of jumping up and down, screaming, "Woo-hoo!"

"Sounds like you were serious about her."

"I asked her to marry me." He rubbed his thumb over his forehead. "In retrospect, not a great idea."

"It must have felt like the right thing to do at the time." By some miracle she sounded calm and wise when she was actually insanely jealous of a woman she didn't know because a man she'd only just met loved that woman enough to want to spend the rest of his life with her. Even if he only thought he did.

"She was right, though. I only asked her because I could feel her pulling away subconsciously, and I guess I panicked."

"Then it's good she said no."

"Yes." He turned to meet her eyes. "It's really good."

Darcy swallowed, not trusting herself to speak.

Greg had talked marriage a few times, always with that take-it-for-granted-I'm-right air. When the subject came up, Darcy had felt like one of those butterflies pinned to the wall in a museum exhibit.

When she thought about Tyler and marriage, even peripherally and completely ludicrously, those butterflies came to life and sailed in a fluttering whirlwind around her stomach.

Okay. Darcy had officially lost it.

She untangled her fingers from Tyler's and jumped up, needing to put sanity space between them. "Let's ride the train."

"I'm there." He fell into step beside her. Their hands bumped and he managed to hold hers again and she managed to let him. "I love that train. My mom claims I said my first sentence after riding it."

"What did you say?"

"'More choo-choo.' Gifted, wasn't I?"

"Genius." She felt weirdly tender imagining Tyler as a little blond boy running around this very zoo. "Where do your parents live?"

"They moved to Shorewood just north of the Milwaukee city line ten years ago, after I graduated college."

"You're lucky. I miss my dad fiercely. Don't remember enough about Mom, but I miss her anyway. I remember her reading to me. I remember warmth and comfort around her, how soft and dark her hair was, that she had glasses and a loud laugh. Not nearly enough."

"You can borrow my parents anytime you want." He started to say something and then apparently changed his mind. She wondered if he'd been going to offer to have her meet them. Probably good he didn't. Meeting the families was a sure sign that couples were seriously involved.

The rain had stopped so they stayed dry standing in line for the train with parents and kids and occasional other kid-free adults until the miniature steam engine puffed into the station, whistle blowing. Reluctant passengers got off and the new excited ones got on. Darcy and Tyler squeezed into an empty car, sitting opposite each other on the kid-size benches.

They smiled in that wordless happy way that meant too much, then the whistle blew, the cars jerked and the train moved slowly across the bridge over a pedestrian road where zoo-goers waved cheerily up at them.

"Isn't this enough of an adventure for you? Traveling to all four corners of the Milwaukee County Zoo? From grizzly bears of North America to kangaroos of Australia and polar bears of the Arctic. What more could you want?"

"You're right!" She threw up her hands. "What was I thinking?"

"Tell me more about what you're looking for."

Tell him more. How could she resist? This was a new kind of seduction—of her mind instead of her body. Having sex with him would have been less intimate than this kind of connection, which put her in danger of falling too hard. "New experiences. Trying out different versions of myself in places where no one knows me. Exploring different parts of the country, different attitudes, different cultures, and seeing how I fit."

"You don't fit here?"

"I do. But there might be parts of me that Milwaukee will never reach. I want to find out how much of me exists out of habit, how much of me is defined by the people who know me and expect me to behave in certain ways. I want to find out who I am now that I don't have to identify me with the person I'm taking care of."

"You don't think you'll encounter the same old problems in a new setting?"

"Possibly." She lifted her hands—what can I do? "But then I will have learned that."

He smiled slowly, eyes seeming to drink her in. "You are a remarkable woman, Darcy Wolf."

She opened her mouth to thank him when unexpected tears she refused to let fall decided to make that impossible. She tried again, this time to tell him she thought he was a very remarkable man, but all she managed was, "Yer…mark…too," and a big hiccup.

"Thank you." He touched her knee, grinning, then turned to lean out the window and watch the woods and zoo animals passing.

She watched him instead, his dark blond hair ruffling, his lean body long and easy, folded into the tiny car. Her heart ached until she had to change position on the seat because it seemed as if the beats would stop if she stayed still. She wanted to touch him, taste him. She wanted to take down his jeans, kneel on the floor between his knees, take him into her mouth and completely traumatize the kids and parents watching the train pass and probably get arrested and, okay, so not a good idea. But her hormones were aroused, like little cowboys on horses, galloping and restless, yelling *yeehaw* and *let's go* and *cha-a-a-arge!*

Platonic. Uh-huh. She was doing really well with that.

"Are you excited about teaching this fall?" She needed to get her mind off yet another fantasy and she wanted to know everything about him that she could find out.

"Very. I had my eye on that prize all the way through graduate school."

"I think you'll be a great teacher."

"Why is that?"

"Because you're charismatic and interesting and you listen when people talk to you."

"Why, thank you, Ms. Wolf. I'm flattered."

"It's not flattery. You don't mind coming back to your hometown?"

"Mind? No. Where I live doesn't define me. And I love Wauwatosa and Milwaukee. Could I be happy somewhere else? Sure. But the job is here, my family's here. I still have friends here. Saves me having to put down roots somewhere else." He put his hand on her knee again, gave it a brief tap. "Because, traveling woman, I believe having roots is the most important factor as to whether you're happy in any given place."

"Interesting theory." She wished he hadn't moved his hand off her knee. "I've felt more tied here than rooted."

"Fair enough." The train went around the final curve, slowed and came to a stop at the station, where a new crop of riders waited, children squirming with impatience. Tyler got out first and gallantly offered her a hand she didn't need but took anyway. She stepped on the platform and they followed the small crowd through the low iron exit gate. Several of the kids immediately clamored to go on the merry-go-round. Darcy wasn't one of them. Merry-go-rounds made her ill.

"So in the weeks you have left, will you be visiting Starlight City again?"

"Oh." She found herself grateful for the cool breeze because she was blushing. *Way to be a wild woman of the world, Darcy.* "No, I'm done with that. It wasn't what I expected."

"No more fantasy fulfillment?"

She frowned. When had she told him that was her fantasy? "I don't know. I do have more fantasies, though."

"Care to share?"

She sent him a reprimanding look. "Privileged information."

"Of course, sorry." Except he didn't look sorry. He was smiling at her, and as he was smiling at her the clouds parted just for a second and a sunbeam came out of nowhere and lit him up as if God were saying, "Darcy, I picked this one out for you. Don't you dare screw it up."

Oh, boy.

"Ready for home?"

She nodded, stomach jumbled with a mixture of relief and disappointment. But it was just as well. The more she was with him, the more she felt herself developing an attachment, the way mussels spin out sticky threads one by one until they're firmly anchored wherever they choose. She'd been firmly anchored here too long. Time to break free and swim with the tides.

As she had said so often, it was starting to feel as if she were trying to convince herself.

They drove home in silence. Darcy sneaked peeks at Tyler once in a while, pretending to be checking out businesses on Blue Mound Road, like Big Apple Bagels. My, how fascinating. Actually she was wondering what he was thinking. His face was neutral, hands relaxed on the wheel.

She knew what she was thinking. She was thinking she'd like to wrap herself around him so he'd have to drag her clinging body everywhere he went for the rest of his life.

But then she'd never make it to Seattle or Los Angeles or Miami or Boston and she'd spend the rest of her life wondering what she could have learned and what adventures she might have had that would have changed or enriched her before she settled down.

"You can drop me at your house. You don't need to drive me home."

"Sure I do."

"No, really. I want to go back to my walk anyway."

"A mile or so around the zoo wasn't enough?"

"More won't hurt." She actually wanted to avoid going home, because once she was back she'd start brooding and might never stop.

"As you like it." He pulled into his driveway and the garage. They got out of the car and walked grimly to the house. Obviously neither of them wanted the day to end.

"Thanks for coming with me, Darcy."

She took his outstretched hand for a solemn shake, and then neither of them wanted to let go so neither of them did. "Thanks for inviting me. I love the zoo. It was really fun."

"It was." He released her hand, which made her want to grab it and shove hers back where it belonged. "Have a good walk."

"Thanks." That was her cue so she walked a few steps then turned to wave. He was standing watching her with his hands on his hips, face very serious. When he saw her wave, he smiled and waved back and then he went inside and his door closed.

Thud.

Damn it.

She took two steps back toward his door, then two more, then three, then there she was, standing with her hand ready to reach for the bell.

Except she couldn't ask him for more when she had nothing to give him in return except another right-now, and that was manipulative and sleazy of her. She should march right back up to Clarke Street and continue on her way as if none of this afternoon had happened.

But it had happened and the glow was still with her. She'd be a nifty night-light for any child's room.

Leave. She glared down at her feet. Leave. Leave-leave-leave.

Nothing. But neither did her hand reach for the doorbell.

Classic indecision.

She'd close her eyes and count to three and then she'd leave.

One. Two. Thr—

The door flew open, a male hand reached for her and dragged her inside and up against his solid chest, where he proceeded to kiss her so thoroughly that she decided no one had ever kissed her before, because this completely replaced their silly amateur attempts.

Her whole body came alive, her mind felt clear and light and joyous. He might have pulled her in, but this was what she'd wanted all along, and how stupid she'd been to pretend otherwise. She fumbled with his shirt, he fumbled with hers, and then they were both topless, skin to skin and starting the fumble-fumble with the rest of their clothes, kissing desperately whenever they could.

She hadn't ever, ever been this turned on before.

Then he pressed her against the wall with his big body and his erection sought the place it liked best, only that pose wasn't really feasible. So she lifted her leg and he kind of bent his knees and they almost got it right, but who could stay like that for very long? Then he tried lifting her, and he was plenty strong enough, but even an Olympic weightlifter would have trouble keeping one hundred and twenty-five pounds of very odd-shaped weight aloft and moving back and forth to climax. So that didn't work well either. Wrapping her legs around his waist helped with the weight, but who could move on and off a magnificent erection with legs gripping that tightly?

Not her.

Perhaps the kama sutra was written for circus performers.

"Wait." She laid a hand on his chest, slid to the floor and knelt at his feet. "I have a better idea."

She took him into her mouth as she'd been fantasizing about on the train, and from his low moans of contentment, she'd gather that he thought it was a better idea, too.

Darcy wasn't usually first in line for this type of activity. As one girlfriend had said, hootingly, it wasn't called a "blow fun."

But for this man she was suddenly an expert and ravenous for him. He was a perfect size, tasted clean and male, and she grew desperately aroused again even though he was getting all the benefits. She glanced up and found him watching her, his eyes bright with passion, lips parted. She felt as if she were starring in their own personal porn video, tasteful of course, and very, very exciting.

So she ramped up her talents, ran her hands up his legs, stroked and manipulated his testicles, finding out where and how he liked to be touched best.

Everywhere and any way, it seemed.

All the while she was more and more excited by how excited she was making him, and it didn't matter that he was getting all the stimulation because his pleasure had become hers.

So when he tried to pull out she insisted he stay in, holding his hips briefly to make her point, and sucked harder, used her hand at the base of his cock to help, sensing he was close, putting all her energy into making him come because she wanted so desperately for him to have that from her lips.

And when he did, she experienced a surge of pleasure so complete that she might as well have come herself.

"Darcy." He sank to his knees, put his arms around her and rested his cheek against hers, so that she felt completely enclosed by his affection and did her best to show how much she returned it. If affection was the right word, which it didn't seem to be, but best not to think about that now.

He unwrapped his arms and pushed her gently back. "Let me—"

"No, you don't have to."

"Have to?" He quirked an eyebrow and smiled mischievously. "What part of touching you could ever be a duty?"

"I don't—"

"Shh. Lie back. Enjoy."

She did. And ohhh, she did. And it seemed at the end that she wasn't having a vaginal orgasm or a clitoral orgasm, but an emotional orgasm, because the rush of ecstasy seemed to be centered in her heart. And when she came down from the considerable height, he was there, catching her from the fall. He kissed her and gazed at her and she gazed back with as much warmth and affection—or whatever—as he was showing her.

"Darcy."

"Mmm." Even the happy sated sound was an effort. She was jellylike with afterglow.

"Do me a favor?"

"Mmm?"

"Don't leave suddenly or tell me to stay away again."

His eyes held hers while her body moved restlessly. *Don't try to trap me* was her first thought. Then her second was very different.

"No. I won't. I promise." The words exited her lips before she'd even thought them. Or maybe they just hadn't bothered asking her brain for permission they knew her fear would deny.

No question, she was in trouble.

Serious, serious trouble.

10

"I SWEAR, there's not a single piece of sexy underwear in here that doesn't make me look like a water buffalo." Molly indicated the beautiful but unflattering negligee she'd tried on in a Victoria's Secret dressing room. "Make that a water buffalo with PMS who ate salty food and has bad gas."

"That's not your color. The stark white washes you out." Darcy held up another hanger on which floated a graceful nightgown in a pretty shade of peach. "Try this."

"It's not the color. It's the fact that I don't weigh eighty-two pounds."

"Because you're not twelve. Try this one."

"It's no use." Molly slumped down on the stool in the dressing room and gazed disgustedly in the mirror, where her defeated posture made the lovely gown look even worse. "I can't compete with Ms. Solid Muscle. I weigh one-forty. She probably weighs—"

"You're not competing. She's not even in the race. Come on. Try this one. Bruce will get a hard-on just looking at the label."

"So show him the label. He can have sex with that and I'll put on sweatpants and eat a pound of Oreos in the corner."

"Molly…"

Molly sighed and stood to take off the clingy white nightie, which regained its sex appeal once it was safely back on the hanger. "Okay, okay. But this is an exercise in futility. Not to mention humility."

"Here." Darcy held the peach gown out insistently. "This has an empire waist, it's not too short and it has great cleavage potential."

"Perfect for my grandmother."

"Not even close. You'll look stunning."

Molly slid the nightgown over her blond head and adjusted the straps, examining herself critically. "Hmm. Not quite a nightmare this time. More like your garden-variety bad dream."

"Ha!" Darcy clapped her hands together. Molly looked fabulous, and how. All the health the white gown had drained from her skin had flooded right back in. "That's it. You look totally hot. Your new haircut makes your neck yards long, the fullness of the nightie de-emphasizes what no healthy woman wants emphasized, and you look completely boobilicious where it counts."

Molly scowled to cover her pleasure. "I need the personal trainer, not Bruce. Look at those flabby arms."

"Forget it. The color's perfect. The fit is perfect. You look very sexy and Bruce will go wild. We're taking it."

"Only five hundred ensembles later." Molly turned side to side in front of the mirror with a small smile. "I guess it's not too bad. Why aren't you getting anything?"

Darcy snorted. "What for?"

"Ohhh, gee, I dunno, maybe...*Tyler?*"

"Uh, no."

"Why not?"

"You want to know the truth?"

"No, I want you to lie to me." Molly started to take off the nightgown. "Of course I want the truth."

"I don't want lingerie for him, because I'm—"

"I swear, if you start with the keep-him-at-arm's-length-because-you're-leaving thing again, I'll—"

"Because I'm never in clothes long enough for him to see it."

Molly burst out laughing with the nightgown over her head,

which made her look like a shaking peach-colored tent. "Okay, that works for me. So when's your next date?"

"Tomorrow night."

"And? What are you doing?"

"Dinner at that Ethiopian restaurant on Farwell."

"Oh, you are so lucky. We still can't go anywhere that doesn't serve mac 'n' cheese or pizza."

"Yes, you can." Darcy arranged Molly's new nightie on the hanger and hung it on a hook while her friend dressed. "I adore your kids. I'll babysit. You and Bruce should go out."

"He's out plenty already. With whatsername."

Darcy put her hands on her hips. Enough. Her friend was off the deep end without a flotation device. "I can't believe how defeatist you're being. Where's Molly the fighter? The one who took on the school board that year second-grade classes were way overcrowded. How about the one who helped campaign for smoke-free restaurants in Wauwatosa? Or the one who—"

"I'm too scared to fight, Darce." Molly bit her lips, suddenly near tears. "What if I lose?"

Darcy gaped at her. "What, so you're going to sit back and let her take him?"

"I thought you claimed there was no danger of that."

"I can't imagine there is. But what do I know?"

"Thanks." Molly stepped into her shoes as if they needed punishment. "That's incredibly comforting."

"I'm not saying anything you haven't tortured yourself with already. I know firsthand how powerful fantasies are. Not to mention the thrill of the forbidden."

"Tyler's not forbidden. Far from it."

"In a way he is, since I'm leaving. The more I tell myself I can't have Tyler, the more I want him. I'm sure it's the same with Bruce and whatsername."

Darcy's voice dropped on the last word. She turned away so

Molly wouldn't see her face. Why had she just said that? Did she believe it, really? Were all these wild feelings for Tyler merely the excitement of forbidden fruit? And why should that upset her, when it would make her life easier to think of him that way, really?

Except she didn't want to. And didn't want to examine why not either.

Oh, what fun.

"You and Tyler have a lot more going for you than fantasy and thrills."

"Oh, come on." Her heart leaped at the thought and she had to tell it to stick to pumping blood, thanks very much. "I don't know that any more than you know what's going through Bruce's mind. Which brings up the obvious next question— why don't you ask him?"

"Because either way, I lose. Either he realizes I don't trust him, which is really bad and possibly damaging, or I find out something I'd much rather not know, which is extremely bad and horrendously damaging. That's why I thought…" Her voice faltered. She wiped her eyes, picked up her large black purse and gestured hopelessly toward the peach gown. "I hoped I'd be able to tell tonight, depending on how he reacted to a seduction. Our sex life has never dropped off before this. Never. It's like he's not interested anymore."

"I can't believe that—"

"Let's face it." She took a long, shuddering breath. "After only eight years, my marriage depends on this nightgown."

"Now you're being melodramatic."

"Maybe." Molly shrugged. "But after you and Tyler have been married for a while, you'll see what I mean."

"Oh, that's encouraging." Darcy raised her hand and let it slap down on her thigh, ignoring the adrenaline buzz at the idea of marrying Tyler. "That just makes me want to *rush* down the aisle. Unfortunately we'll have to postpone the ceremony because I'm—"

"Leaving, I know. I wish you'd rethink that."

"Really? You've never mentioned it."

"Look what you're giving up by going." Molly grabbed Darcy's arm and made her turn to face her. "You'll be lonely as hell in those new places. Someone like Tyler doesn't come along every day."

"Oh, so I should chain myself to the first sucker I can possibly land because hell hath no horror like a woman without a man?" She pulled her arm free, more irritated than she should be, and banged through the dressing room door. "I don't think so."

"What about the companionship, the support, the—"

"Suspicion, the mistrust, the heartbreak. Oo-oh, baby, sign me up."

"Wait." Molly ran a few steps to catch up with Darcy's angry strides. "Even if the worst is true and Bruce is into this woman, I know this is only a blip on the radar screen of our lifelong commitment to—"

"Really? A second ago your marriage's last hope of rescue from total destruction was Super Nightie." She poked at the peach rayon hanging from Molly's arm. "And while we're at it, why is it that married women do nothing but complain about their husbands on the one hand, and try to match up all their single friends on the other? Misery loves company?"

Molly stopped short at the register and handed the nightgown to the smiling salesclerk. "Don't be ridiculous."

"Look." Darcy whipped out her cell. "I'm sick of this. Call Bruce right now and ask him. Just ask him. Are you having an affair?"

The salesgirl's smile drooped into shock.

"I can't."

"Then I will."

"Darcy…" Molly looked at her pleadingly, but she made no move to stop Darcy dialing Bruce's cell, which gave Darcy all the permission she needed.

The phone rang. Once. Twice.

"Hel-lo-o? Bruce Johnston's phone." The female voice was low, throaty, unbearably sexy.

"Uh." Darcy glanced nervously at Molly. In the background she heard a man's voice moaning in ecstasy. "Is Bruce there?"

"Bruce can't come to the phone right now." The sex vixen chuckled deep in her throat. "Is it important?"

In the background again, Bruce's voice. *Oh, God, that's good. Ohhh. Don't stop. You're incredible.*

Darcy felt sick. "I…I…uh…"

"Oh, dear God. What is it? Why do you look like that?" Molly grabbed the cell and put it to her ear, holding her arm out to fend Darcy off as she tried to grab the phone back.

The salesgirl announced the total for the nightgown, looking between Darcy and Molly in bewilderment.

Molly gasped; her eyes widened. She listened for a couple more seconds, then punched off the phone. "Oh, God, Darcy. I think he was having an orgasm."

The salesgirl took a step back and plaintively repeated the total Molly owed. Twice.

"No. No, I'm sure he wasn't. She was just giving him a massage or something."

"Is that supposed to make me feel better?"

"Molly, be reasonable. Why would she answer the phone if they were having sex? And if he knew she was on the phone, why would he continue to make loud noises that were bound to be heard?"

"I don't know. Maybe he's into kinky stuff now."

The salesgirl cleared her throat. "Excuse me?"

"Listen to yourself, Moll. You're making yourself nuts over

nothing. Pay for the nightgown, wear it for him tonight. His response will tell you everything you need to know. I'm not a betting woman, but I'd give huge odds in favor of him attacking you with everything he's got."

"Everything he's got left over from Lolita."

Darcy made a face. "She's that young?"

"No. Her name is actually Lolita. Can you stand it?"

"Oh, my God!" Darcy gave a shout of laughter. "Arrest her parents. That's child abuse."

"Excuse me? Please?" The salesgirl's voice had climbed higher. "There are other customers in line?"

Darcy took pity and motioned to the salesgirl. "Pay the woman, Molly."

"Oh. Right. Sorry." Molly dug in her purse for her credit card and put the salesgirl's smile back on her face by handing it over, then signing the slip.

"Thank you! Come again!"

"Let's go." Darcy picked up the bag and tossed it to Molly. "Next stop, Cold Stone Creamery for make-us-feel-better sundaes."

"This close to dinner?"

"Pleez. Stop being a mom. Be a woman."

"I'll get womanly bulges under my nightgown."

"Nonsense. The calories will fortify you." She dragged her friend to the ice cream store, where they ordered a waffle bowl sundae with peanut butter cups and hot fudge—to share, but just because Molly insisted.

They found a table easily because only completely decadent people or those in deep despair would eat ice cream at 5:00 p.m. on a chilly Thursday.

Darcy ate a few distracted spoonfuls, trying to think of a way to help Molly. Her friend didn't deserve any pain in her life. She was always such an angel when Darcy needed—

Click! Lightbulb! *Angel!*

"I've been thinking…"

"Uh-oh." Molly peered at Darcy in mock apprehension.

"…that tonight when you seduce Bruce, you have to pretend to yourself that you're someone else."

Molly's eyebrows shot up. "Why?"

"Maybe Bruce needs to see you in a new light. Maybe he needs to remember back when you were his ultimate fantasy."

"During the Dark Ages?"

"During the dating ages."

"Mmm." She sighed mournfully. "That would be nice."

"Do what I did when I went to Starlight City. Think up a new name for yourself, a new identity. It frees you to behave differently."

"Hmm…" Molly shoved in a huge bite of vanilla, peanut butter and chocolate. "How about…Molita?"

Darcy put her hand over her mouth to keep from spitting ice cream. "Uh, how about not?"

"I've always loved the name Dahlia."

"Done." Darcy smacked the table triumphantly. "Tonight, when you put the nightgown on, you're not Molly. You're *La Belle Dahlia, ooh la la.* Who is ten times sexier than Lolita. No, eleven times."

"Eleven, wow."

"Take a nice bath, do your hair, put on makeup and his favorite perfume, and then…" She winked. "Do something he doesn't expect."

"Remember to take my razor off the edge of the tub?"

"Oh, yeah." Darcy made a sound of exasperation. "That'll make him shoot right into ecstasy."

"You'd be surprised."

Darcy snorted. "Are you trying to sell relationships or talk me out of them?"

"Both." She smiled sadly. "I don't know, Darcy. I love Bruce, but off the record, there are some things I miss about being single."

"Like…?"

"The excitement, the possibilities, the freedom, the…"

"Fantasies?"

"Yeah." Molly dipped her spoon again. "Those."

"I'm sure that's normal." She was very sure. But she felt sick hearing it from Molly's lips. Love precluded fantasy and excitement? There was no way to have both? She wanted it all. Eventually.

"I'm just saying. Everything has its good and bad sides, the yin and yang of life."

Darcy licked a trace of fudge off her spoon and let it drop back on the plate, no longer in the mood for fat and sugar. "If you had it to do over, would you?"

"Marry Bruce? Absolutely. I've been really happy. Although if I had everything to do over…" She gazed off in the distance. "I probably wouldn't have gotten married at eighteen. I would have played more first. I would have taken the time to—"

Her spoon froze midair. She refocused and stared at Darcy in alarm.

"Travel?" Darcy said innocently. "Live in a new town? Explore new sides of yourself? Indulge yourself with some of those fantasies while you still could?"

"Aw, hell. Did I stick my foot in it or what?" Molly laid her spoon on the table and pushed the waffle bowl toward Darcy.

"Well?"

"Okay, okay." Molly put her hands up in surrender. "You win. I would have. I would have done all of that…and then some."

11

TYLER FINISHED PRIMING his last window of the day on a 73rd Street duplex. Quitting time. He'd go home and shower, maybe whip up a batch of Chinese dumplings for dinner. He also had some bok choy, which he could sauté with garlic, ginger and a touch of soy sauce, a perfect accompaniment.

The meal sounded so good his stomach growled. Did Darcy like Chinese food? They had a date the following evening at an Ethiopian place, a relative newcomer to the Milwaukee food scene, which had evolved considerably since his youth. Maybe he should invite Darcy over to dinner tonight, too. She'd promised she wouldn't push him away anymore, so he had every right to call her. Every right to see her. Every right to fall faster and harder.

But did he have any right to try to convince her not to leave town in two weeks? His impression of Darcy was that if she really wanted to go, nothing would stop her. Molly seemed to think whatever Darcy was searching for wouldn't be found just by trading scenery. If that were true, Darcy probably needed to learn that for herself, but he wished she'd figure it out soon. Like tomorrow. Two weeks was too soon to know exactly where their relationship was destined to end up. If someone asked him now, based on the initial rush of feelings, he'd say yes, they had what it took to go the distance. But he couldn't trust those feelings. Could he? His sister would say he could.

Back home after skipping the long detour he usually took on his bike to get more exercise, he showered and went straight to the phone.

A machine picked up at Darcy's home number. He didn't bother leaving a message, but dialed her cell. Several rings, then voice mail. Wherever she was, she had her phone off. Driving, maybe, or catching the early show of a movie? She'd said she was going shopping with Molly. Who knew how long that would take? If he could be permitted a sexist eye-roll.

In the kitchen he got out ground turkey—not authentic, but less fatty than pork—and added scallions, ginger, chopped spinach, soy sauce, sesame oil and a little sugar, then sat to stuff the mixture into wonton wrappers for eventual pan-frying.

Three days since their zoo date and he was still on cloud nine. Or ten. Or eleven. How high did clouds go? As far as he was concerned, seeing her every day wouldn't be enough, but conscious of her don't-fence-me-in mentality, he'd decided to back off once he extracted her promise that she wouldn't. If he moved in hard now, she might change her mind.

Which hadn't stopped him from calling her every night and talking until his throat got tired. Long conversations about anything and everything, their childhoods, religion, politics, food, entertainment. The more he got of her, the more he wanted. He'd reached a point in this all-consuming infatuation where he'd toyed with the idea of calling his sister to eat crow, baked, boiled or fried. If this was how Katie felt about Edwin this soon after they met, Tyler couldn't blame her for believing in love at first sight or for thinking they had what it took to marry so soon.

Where were Mr. Practical and his clone, Mr. Sensible? Darcy had turned him over and over until he no longer knew which way was up.

The last dumpling neatly formed, he heated canola oil in two large frying pans and called Darcy again. No answer, and he'd made enough food for two. Looked like he had a big dinner ahead of him.

He browned the dumplings on one side, then turned them over and poured two-thirds of a cup of water into each pan, covered them, lowered the heat and set the kitchen timer for twelve minutes. While the dumplings steamed, he chopped bok choy and seasonings and put that to braise, then opened a well-deserved beer.

One sip later, out of nowhere came the certainty that he should call Katie right then. He missed her and he now had the perfect way to extend the olive branch—by groveling.

His sister answered on the second ring. "Tyler. What's happened? Are Mom and Dad okay?"

His mouth twisted involuntarily. Their relationship had become so strained that she thought he'd only call to report a tragedy. "They're fine. I actually called to say hi."

"Really?" She obviously didn't buy that one.

"We've been… Things have been rough between us recently."

"More than recently."

A twinge of irritation he couldn't help. "Okay, things have been rough between us more than recently. Happy?"

"What do you want, Tyler?"

This was not going well. "I wanted to talk to you about… love at first sight."

"Come on. Haven't we done this enough by now? Seriously, you've made yourself perfectly clear on the topic and I don't appreciate you calling now to try to dig up all that crap again and throw it in my—"

"Whoa, whoa, *whoa* there. Back up. Let me finish."

She exhaled in annoyance. "Fine. Go ahead."

He sneaked a sip of beer. She was not making this easy. "Look. I've thought a lot about what you said lately. Because…"

His mouth was open, but the words weren't coming. Apparently he really hated the taste of crow.

"Because?"

"I…met someone."

"And…?"

"And, so…"

"Sooo?" He could hear the wheels turning in her head, knew she'd already put the pieces together but just wanted to make him say it.

"You're enjoying this, aren't you?"

"Tremendously. Keep going."

"Sooo I think there might just possibly be a minuscule random something or other to what you said."

"I'm sorry, I didn't have my tape recorder on. Could you repeat that?"

"Not in a million years."

His sister chuckled and he felt a stirring of hope that they could get past their years-long alienation. He'd have Darcy to thank for that.

"I take it you fell for someone with a bang?"

"Big one, yeah." He braced himself for humiliation and instead felt only relief at being able to say it. "It makes no sense."

"Of course it doesn't. Why do you think poets and novelists and playwrights and screenwriters have been obsessed with love for centuries? No one writes about two plus two equaling four because it's easily proved and universally accepted. But love…it's not explainable or definable even after decades of progress in science and psychology."

"True." He still hated the whole gooey-mystical aspect. "So it's not just testosterone in overdrive?"

"I'm sure that's part of it, you gigolo. I've felt that pure, amazingly powerful lust before. But when I met Edwin... Well, I've told you. You and I have argued it out forever."

Tyler took the lids off the dumplings. "But I'm really listening now, Katie."

"What? I presented my side so brilliantly all those times for nothing?" She made a noise of exasperation. "Okay. For the millionth time, here goes. You don't only lust for the body, you lust for time together, whatever form it takes."

"Uh-huh." Phone calls night after night, adolescent in length. Check.

"You love her for herself, not just for the way she makes you feel."

"Sure, okay, right." That much was true; he admired her immensely. Check.

"Everything you do together is new and exciting and wonderful, even if it's taking out trash."

"Uh, right." He started feeling uncomfortable with all this stuff when it involved his emotions instead of Katie's. But yeah, check. Even trash.

"And you're absolutely sure looking ahead at all the years of your life that no matter how much you want to strangle her at any given point, you'll never, ever have a time when you won't love her and want to be with her."

"Something like that." He started flipping dumplings onto a plate. This was getting a little girly touchy-feely for him.

"You've been hit. Oh, this is total justice. Wait until I tell Edwin." Katie sighed blissfully. "Tell me about her."

"She grew up here in Tosa. I vaguely remember her as one of the girls hanging around Cam."

"Ha! If you remember one out of that billion, you're truly destined for each other. Tell me more."

"She's smart, funny, sexy, energetic, beautiful..." His throat thickened. He was definitely losing it.

"Listen to you! Oh, this is too much fun." She giggled and Tyler gritted his teeth. "So when are you going to ask her to marry you?"

"I'm not. She's leaving town in two weeks." He stacked the last dumpling on the pile and tipped the just-wilted bok choy into a bowl.

"What? Oh, no!" His sister sounded even more distressed than he felt. "Why?"

"She has plans to live in the four corners of the country and find herself. Seattle, Los Angeles, Miami and Boston."

"How long are we talking, a year?"

"Eight."

"*Eight years?* Oh, this is bad. You can't let her go."

He put the loaded plates of food on his table. "Katie, I'm not her keeper."

"You want her to go?"

"Of course I don't. It's going to kill me."

"Then…it's easy."

"What is?" His hopes rose in spite of himself.

"Ask her to marry you, she'll say yes, and then she won't go."

He rolled his eyes and sat, remembered his beer and got up again. "Is everything that simple in your little world?"

"Hey, back off."

His grin didn't last. "I haven't known her long enough to ask her."

"Says who?"

"I barely know her at all."

"And?"

"I don't think marrying someone you don't know is a great idea."

"You knew Annie. Look how that turned out."

Tyler closed his eyes. He hated when something he knew to be completely idiotic started to make sense. "Marriage is a huge step."

"All it takes is love and commitment. Shared values and habits don't hurt. Good sex is a must, but I am pretty sure you wouldn't be walking on air if that wasn't working well."

"No comment."

"I'm happy for you, Tyler." Her voice was low and warm. "I really am."

"Thanks, Katie." He moved back to the kitchen table with his beer and looked out at the fence around Darcy's yard. "I've…missed you."

"Wow. You really are in love. You never would have said anything like that when you were dating Annie. You were so closed off and self-protective."

"I was not." He was. He was sure of it. "Okay, maybe."

"I missed you, too, Shoelace."

He grinned at the old joke, born when they were learning to "Ty" their shoes. "I will probably never forgive you for being right, however."

"You can be right next time, 'kay?" She laughed again, laughter he'd missed a lot. "Promise me you won't let this one get away."

He rolled his eyes again. "*Et tu*, Katie?"

"What do you mean?"

"Annie said the same thing."

"Annie did?"

"She's back in town. We had dinner."

"Well, then you know it's right. Check with Mom, and if she agrees, then the three women next in importance behind— Tell me her name?"

"Darcy."

"The three women most important in your life besides Darcy can't be wrong. Wait. Darcy Wolf?"

"Yes."

"I know her! We were in summer track together during high

school my senior year. I love Darcy. Okay, that settles it. Go buy the ring and ask her. I guarantee she'll stay to marry you. Or at very least leave town for only a few months with your rock on her finger."

"Wow." Tyler sat at the table, feeling split by her chatter. His heart was doing college-level rah-rah cheers. His brain was setting off deafening wait-a-second alarm bells. "But I don't see how—"

"Live large. Be like Cam. Take a risk. It'll pay off. And if you don't, guess what? You'll spend the rest of your life miserable because you didn't try to stop her."

"Katie…" His heart did a flashy somersault and landed in a split; his brain indicated he was about to enter the danger zone and to prepare for total annihilation. "Rushing into marriage isn't smart."

"Two years later, I'm so happy with Edwin it isn't even funny. You and Annie didn't work out and you gave that tons of time. If I'd done the sensible thing, I'd still be in that god-awful job working for Mr. Butthead Lawyer, and I'd be spending every waking minute wondering what I gave up. When it's right, it's right, and you just know. Why waste time making sure of something you are already sure of?"

"But marriage…" He was losing. His objections were starting to sound feeble and repetitive. The cheering squad had turned into an Olympic gymnastics team.

"Has Darcy had other relationships that didn't work out?"

He poured soy sauce, rice vinegar and chili oil over the mountain of dumplings. "Who hasn't?"

"Good. So she'll know this is different, too. And she'll want to know how serious you are about her. If you don't ask, Shoelace, you won't be giving her enough to stay for."

"You really are—" His line beeped. Call waiting. He was almost relieved. He needed time away from Katie's arguments and his backflipping heart to reestablish contact with his brain. "I have to go. Another call."

"Promise me you'll think about it?"

"Promise." Like he'd think about anything else every minute until Darcy either left or stayed?

"Bye, big brother. Take care. I'll call you soon, okay?"

Tyler smiled, momentarily choked up. "That would be great, little sister."

He clicked over to the other call, still smiling, and stuffed in a dumpling before they got cold. It was really, really good to talk to Katie. And he really, really needed some time to sit and think about what she'd said, because he wasn't sure scheming to keep Darcy here was smart at all. In fact, it could be horrendously selfish.

"Tyler! My man!"

"Hey, Bruce." He took a hurried sip of beer to wash down the dumpling. "What's going on? You going to any Brewers games this summer?"

"Is the sky blue? I'll get us tickets. You name the day."

"I'll check my social calendar and get back to you."

"Gotta ask permission from the little woman, huh?"

"Ha! I'm *way* too much of a manly man for that." He grinned, knowing Bruce understood.

"So, uh, listen, about Darcy…"

Tyler's grin faded. "Uh-oh. Now what?"

"This fantasy thing…"

Tyler put his beer down, energy leaking out of him like air from a punctured tire. "Don't tell me she's going to another bar to pick up men."

"No. Not that bad. But I guess Molly said something and Darcy decided she needed to do this. Molly's terrified she'll be arrested."

He shot to standing. *"Arrested?"*

"She's going to the art museum to, uh, whack off. Or whatever women say."

"In a public bathroom?"

"Forget the bathroom. In public."

"In—" He was split again. One half was shocked. The other half formed an instant picture of Darcy's aroused face and her hand under her skirt, and he started getting hard. "Ho-ly shit."

"Er, so, Molly thinks you need to go and, uh…"

"Help her out?"

"I swear, Molly has to call you next time, man. This is killing me. I guess make sure the guards don't see her, I don't know. I'm the messenger. Though I do love Darcy enough not to want to read about her in the *Journal Sentinel* tomorrow."

"Tomorrow's paper? She's there now? When did she leave?" He immediately started calculating how long it would take to drive downtown.

"Not yet. She's heading over in about half an hour. Museum's open until eight tonight. She and Molly just finished shopping. Molly called me from a mall bathroom, for God's sake. She didn't have your number, she said, though I think she just wanted me to do the dirty work."

Tyler slapped his hand to his forehead, drew it down over his face. Was this his life? Really? Or was this happening to someone else? What on earth had possessed her? "Okay. I'll go."

"Sorry, man."

"One thing, Bruce. What the hell could Molly have said that would make Darcy immediately want to run to a museum to…do that?"

"Uh. Well. Molly said she wished she'd taken a lot more time to have fun before she married me."

Tyler thudded back down into his chair. More fun before she got married. And whoosh, Darcy rushed right off to start. What had he been thinking? A woman ready for marriage wouldn't have been inspired to bring herself off in public. At least he didn't think so. "Ouch."

Bruce cleared his throat. "I don't know, man. I think something's up with Molly. She's acting very…not herself."

"Molly?" Tyler dragged himself far enough out of his own shock to listen to his friend. "How so?"

"Like, she doesn't want to…host the wiener, you know?"

"Host the wiener?" Tyler held the phone away from his ear for a second, grimacing. He hoped he'd misheard. "You have got to be—"

"C'mon, man, this is bad stuff. We've never had this problem before."

"Okay. Okay, I'm sorry." Tyler grabbed his beer as if it were lifesaving medicine. "I don't have any advice other than to talk to her. I don't even know which way is up in my own relationship, and you've had a hell of a lot more experience than I have."

"Yeah, I know. I should just talk to her. I'm kinda scared what she'll say, though. Like maybe she has someone else?" His voice cracked.

"Molly? I can't believe it, Bruce. You guys are made for each other. Just talk to her. I'm sure it's nothing. Maybe some female thing."

"Yeah, maybe." He sighed heavily. "Okay. It'll be fine. You get down to the museum to see the show."

Tyler winced. "Uh, yeah, I'll do that. You stay far away, though, okay?"

"Hmm. I don't know. I'm kinda having a hankering to look at some art myself."

"Talk to your wife, Bruce."

"I'm there, man. Good luck."

"Same to you." He punched off the phone.

Welcome to another chapter of Descent into Madness: The

Darcy and Tyler Story. He'd been considering marriage? This woman wasn't remotely ready to make a commitment of that type. And therefore he shouldn't be, either.

She wanted to go all over the country, seduce more workmen, pick up more strangers in bars, have orgasms in multiple national monuments. Or maybe multiple orgasms in one national monument. Either way, he was glad Bruce had called. Glad to be pulled down from the love-at-first-sight woowoo stuff his sister was trying to pull over on him.

His path was now clear.

He'd drive to the art museum, make sure Darcy didn't get arrested, and then…

As much as it might kill him, he'd have to let her go.

12

Darcy parked her car on the little road at the end of the museum driveway by the restaurant Pieces of Eight, where another car had miraculously just pulled out. She preferred that area to the underground garage so on the short walk to the entrance she could enjoy fresh air and light. Not to mention the gorgeous view of the great white sunshade wings that swept skyward from the museum's recent addition, architect Santiago Calatrava's genius contribution to the lakefront.

She locked her yellow Beetle and stood smiling in the chilly breeze that swept off the water, feeling an unexpected pang of love for her native city, which she was so anxious to leave. Cool again today, summer seemed much farther off than it was on the calendar. But at least the sun was out, though on its way to setting, and the waves sparkled blue, deepening to navy toward the horizon.

This was going to be fun.

Car keys dropped into her purse, she crossed the grassy lawn toward the beckoning lake. The breeze ruffled her hair and tickled between her legs, where its coolness focused attention on her lack of panties.

Shameless. Truly.

She grinned and put on her sunglasses, less for relief from the glare than from a need to feel slightly more anonymous, slightly more mysterious. Not her, embarking on this adventure, not Darcy but *Veronique,* pronounced with a delicious French accent. *Mon Dieu, oui.* Because even though she wasn't French and had never been to France, Darcy imagined that everyone in Europe was delightfully free of inhibitions, and if they came across her pleasuring herself in public they'd only say, *"Oh, pardon, madame,"* while Americans would call the police and condemn her to hell. Probably both at the same time.

A friend who'd moved to Austria had sent her an article about a local museum that offered free admission to anyone who showed up naked. What's more, people took advantage, which had tickled her about as much as the wind off the lake. Darcy couldn't imagine anyone in the Midwest sponsoring a Naked Night Out. Maybe she should look into it, though most people looked better with clothes on, now that she thought about it.

The lake was beautiful, restless and free, and instead of glorying in its power and her own, she immediately wished Tyler were there to share the sight with her.

Sacrebleu! Bad Veronique, bad. Over that waffle bowl of ice cream, one glimpse of Molly's sad and wistful face when she admitted to wishing she'd had more premarital adventures of a wide and occasionally wicked variety had been like a huge hello?-hello?-wake-up call. Molly adored Bruce. He owned her heart. Their marriage, barring the current personal-trainer weirdness, had been healthy and happy. But even *she* wished she'd had more time on her own before settling down.

Voilà. Exactly what Darcy was after, exactly what she needed and why she'd come up with her plan to move around the country and to fulfill some favorite fantasies here before she left. Though sadly, she could only fulfill the ones that were possible in real life. Making Gerard Butler her love slave, for example, would most likely have to stay in her imagination. And what a shame that was.

Of course she had promised not to pull back from Tyler and

that was why this fantasy could still work, even if she was splitting hairs a bit. Just a bit. But no other man need be involved, though her original version did include a hot spectator who got hotter the closer he came to sharing her ecstasy. She hadn't promised not to do something like this, though granted, it had probably never occurred to him she'd try.

Veronique easily brushed off the uncomfortable, slightly queasy feeling this logic gave Darcy, and she turned to strut her stuff up the sloping lawn and back toward the museum, the flared hem of her patterned blue skirt blowing back and forth, but thank goodness not high enough to get her an indecent exposure ticket. At least not yet.

Inside, the white marble Calatrava addition reminded her, as it always did, of a fabulous spaceship. Maybe someday it would look quaint, but now the sloping passageways lined with large windows and white marble ribs still had the look of a far distant future.

She paid admission and made her way, heels tapping on marble, down the corridor toward the old part of the museum, a contrast to the modern addition with its traditional right angles, warm stained wood and parquet flooring.

Eh bien. Now to find the perfect place. On the second floor there were some semiprivate spots overlooking the lake…

Up the stairs then, smiling at people on their way down, and thinking how fun that they had no idea what she had in mind. Unlike them, she had not come for scholarship, or self-improvement, or an unbridled love of artistic creation. At least not on this visit.

Up the next set of stairs from the mezzanine to the second floor. At the landing she turned left, where she remembered a little addendum room to the gallery with a narrow doorway and a chair off to the right, out of view to most visitors.

Ah, oui. She hadn't been here in a while, but the little room was still there, at the end of this larger one displaying modern sculpture and paintings. A couch sat in the center in front of a TV playing an interview with an old woman, who must have close ties either to the museum or to some artist. Darcy was embarrassed to say she hadn't stopped to watch closely on her last visit and she wasn't going to stop and watch closely on this one, either. Was she?

Mais non. A few museum-goers wandered around, a middle-aged couple, a lone woman, and one rather scruffy young man sprawled on the couch watching the interview.

Well. No hottie just waiting for her to begin. *Tant pis.* Too bad.

She stepped into the main room; the man on the couch glanced her way then back at the screen. No one else paid the slightest attention.

Alors…

Another step toward the alcove and the same odd disoriented feeling came over her as it had that night at Starlight City. A disconnection from her reality, unpleasant and nerve-racking.

She tried telling herself that breaking new ground would feel different, which was the whole reason she was trying out that new ground, so she should stop freaking and take a lesson from Nike. Just do it.

Two steps this time and she stopped again. In spite of her brilliant self-encouragement, for an awful second she wanted to run outside, jump back into her car, drive as fast as she could to Tyler's house and beg him to make love to her all night long.

And then? She wouldn't have fulfilled this fantasy and someday she'd end up like Molly, wishing she had.

The kid on the couch glanced at her again, propelling her to march determinedly to the tiny room at the end of the hall. The red-upholstered chair was still there, tucked behind the narrow wall just waiting for her.

She sat, spine straight, hands clasped in her lap. In the bar she'd been able to pound back vodka to ease her nerves. Did she really want to do this?

She leaned over and peeked around the doorway into the gallery. Just entering was a single male, late twenties probably, longish dark hair, the kind of big nose that manages to be sexy, and killer dark eyes. He looked slightly exotic, foreign probably, maybe Italian.

Buonasera, mio bello.

He glanced toward her, caught her staring and did a smiling double take. Darcy barely managed to return the smile before ducking her head back into the little room. *Uh, Darcy?* Wasn't a guy like that the *point* of this exercise? Why the hell was she being such a chicken? Look how she'd been with Tyler that first night. She hadn't hesitated a second, hadn't felt anything but bold, sexually powerful and sure. Now she was a complete basket case.

Come on. Of course she was more nervous in a public building than she had been in her own home. And of course she was more nervous than she'd been at Starlight City because, vodka notwithstanding, bars were where people went to hook up. What she planned to do in this museum wasn't very widely accepted. In fact, it was undoubtedly illegal.

That was all.

Happily, diagnosing the root of the problem also lessened her anxiety, and she made herself lean back in the chair, spread her legs slightly and take a few minutes to get where she needed to be mentally.

Eyes closed, she attempted to bring on the right mood, keeping an ear out for approaching footsteps. Time to get this started, time to build up a portfolio of memories to last her through the years when she'd be a mom and wife like Molly and no longer in a position to experiment quite so much.

Gradually her body relaxed, and as her mind cast around for

suitable erotic material, she landed on Gerard Butler, or rather Gerard Butler landed on her.

Mmm, *très, très bon*.

Her hand crept to the hem of her skirt and she pulled it slowly up, ears still on guard, ready to fling the material back over her legs at a microsecond's notice if she needed to.

Gerard was kissing her, his hand making its way slowly up the path her own was traveling. My, my, my, he was good. He knew every single nuance of what she liked and how she liked it and when. Didn't he?

She grinned and circled her sex with the tip of one finger, imagining them together, concentrating hard. Footsteps in the gallery behind her, but muted, far away, no threat.

Exciting though. Very. Discovery as a distant possibility turned her on. Who knew? See how much she was learning about herself already? Her arousal climbed with the motion of her finger. She moved on from poor disappointed Gerard to the handsome Italian stranger in the gallery, imagined him coming in, seeing her, shocked at first—*Madre del Dio!*—then wildly excited, swelling hugely in his pants. She imagined how she'd look to him, head back over the edge of the chair, lips parted, breathing hard, hand busy, hips straining.

Wait. She leaned over the arm of the chair, wanting another peek into the gallery to see if the striking dark man was still there. Yes. In fact the gallery was empty except for…Alberto, she'd call him, who must have seen her head emerge from around the doorway in his peripheral vision because his head abruptly swung toward her. Their eyes met. Her hand worked harder. This was it, just what she wanted. Her perfect fantasy.

Except she felt no pull, no magic, no chemistry.

Darn it.

He smiled, turned toward her fully. Could he tell what she

was doing? He couldn't possibly. She pulled her head out of sight again to relax and regroup. Footsteps approached. He was coming. She'd be coming. Her fantasy was now, here, perfect…

Except her lust shrank into panic. She withdrew her hand, threw down the hem of her skirt and sat up, gazing at Lake Michigan as if it were her new religion.

"Hi." His voice was high and a bit nasal, not a trace of Italy. All Milwaukee all the time. "Nice view, huh?"

"Oh. Yes." She gestured stupidly toward the water. "The lake is gorgeous from up here."

"Yeah. Yeah." He leaned one arm up against the doorway arch. "So…you like art?"

No, she hated it, and that's why she was here in an art museum. On most occasions. This trip was slightly different.

"Art? I don't know him that well, but he seems nice." Badaboom, cymbal crash.

He looked at her blankly. "What…"

"Sorry, lame joke." Which Tyler would at least have laughed at politely. "Never mind."

"Right." He nodded, obviously still not getting it. "Right. You live around here?"

"In Wauwatosa."

"Tosa, yeah. Great place. My sister's cousin lives there. You know him?"

Oh, my God. When they were passing out brain cells… "Sure. I do."

"Yeah? Wow. He's doing good."

"Glad to hear that." Darcy sighed regretfully. Gorgeous package, worthless present. "Uh…I don't mean to be rude, but I kind of wanted to be alone here, if that's okay."

"Oh, yeah, sure. Nice place to be alone. Maybe I'll see you around."

"Maybe." But she really hoped not.

He left, footsteps echoing, gradually quieter, then gone.

Darcy slumped back in her chair. Whoopee. That was about as erotic as a bikini wax.

She gazed out at the water, mind fumbling for another fantasy to get her back on track. Gerard seemed to be busy all of a sudden, maybe shooting his next movie. She certainly couldn't fantasize about Alberto now that he'd turned out to be sooo *not* Alberto.

Maybe if she got up and walked around for a while, calmed down, enjoyed the exhibits and concentrated on the tickly feeling of air under her skirt.

She didn't move from her chair. Aw, shoot. Mostly she was tired and she wanted to go home. Or no, she wanted to call Tyler to see if he wanted to hang out together, have some dinner and mess up his bed. Maybe she'd picked the wrong day for her fantasy to come true. Maybe fantasies like this worked better if they had time to percolate. She'd driven here right after shopping with Molly. Maybe that was too soon, since she'd only just decided to try for real.

Maybe this whole fantasy thing wasn't working too well for her. Though it had started out more perfectly than she could ever have imagined. Maybe she just got lucky with Tyler.

Maybe, maybe, maybe. Why wasn't anything nice and definite?

For so long circumstances had made all the life decisions for her. Taking care of Dad was a given. College was a given. Taking care of Dad again. Helping Greg recover. She supposed it was normal to make mistakes at first when you were finally in control of your life.

Oh, the irony. All that time she'd spent longing for freedom only to discover freedom carried its own load of responsibility.

She plunked her elbows onto her thighs, rested her chin in her hands. At least the view was nice. At least it was a beautiful day. At least she wasn't in a hospital either as patient or visitor. That should make her feel better.

It didn't.

Footsteps again in the gallery behind her. Oh, no. Approaching. Darcy really did want to be alone this time.

She made a face and considered doing something rude in case it was Not-Alberto and she needed to appear disgusting to him.

Of course it could be someone else entire—

A dark blond head poked around the corner. A smile appeared on its face. "Thought I'd find you here."

Her mouth dropped and at the same time bells of joy started ringing throughout her body. "You? Whah? How?"

"Wow." He indicated the view and the room. "Perfect spot for…what you had in mind."

"But…how did you know what I—" Darcy jammed her hands on her hips. The lightbulb had gone on. Twice. "Molly! That little weasel. She told you about Starlight City, too, didn't she? And here I was, Ms. Stupido, amazed that you happened to show up alone on the same night, same—"

"Hey, she was worried about you. Some creep could have given you trouble at Starlight, and you could have been arrested here."

No leniency for Molly. None. Making sense and being a caring friend was no excuse. "Why didn't she show up herself if she was so worried?"

He gave a slow smile, eyes traveling up and down her skirt. "I guess she thought maybe I'd have more fun."

"Humph." She resisted the instant heat his gaze had sparked. "She did seem *aw*fully interested in every detail of my plans. I thought she wanted to live vicariously."

"Maybe that, too." His gaze moved to her tight white top.

"So why did you show up?" She crossed her arms over her chest. "Just because she ordered you to?"

He crouched next to her chair, eyes warm and sincere. "It's not exactly a hardship to be around you, Darcy."

Ohhh. She kept herself from sighing out loud. The battle against joy and desire was not going at all well. "Really?"

"And the idea of keeping other men away from you in whatever capacity was another real draw." He trailed a finger down her cheek, over her collarbone. "I couldn't stand thinking about you going home with anyone else at Starlight. Or anyone else watching what you were planning to do here."

Drip, drip, drip. Darcy's spring thaw in full force. "Well. Uh. That hasn't really gotten going yet."

"No?" He looked very interested in that fact and also relieved. "How long have you been here?"

"Oh. Well. Long enough. I just... It didn't..." She blew out a frustrated breath hard enough to move the curtain a few feet in front of her.

"Didn't feel right?"

"Yeah. That. I mean, I tried, but...I don't know. Maybe the idea was sexier than the reality."

"Why don't you try again?"

"Oh. But now that you're here, it wouldn't be the same."

His features stilled. "Why not?"

"Because." She tipped her head and gave him a look calculated to un-still his face in a hurry. "You're not a stranger."

"True." His face moved again. In fact it moved quite a bit closer to hers. The space between them became intimate and highly charged. "That didn't bother you at the Starlight."

"Also true." She smiled and he smiled and the arousal that had been banished started slipping back.

"I have an idea." His gaze went on another round-trip excursion of her body. "Close your eyes."

She closed them, unquestioning, hyperaware of him next to her. Whatever he had in mind was fine with her. She trusted him completely. And it suddenly hit her that even if Alberto had been Alberto after all, she wouldn't have reacted this eagerly. Or at all.

"Now pretend you've just arrived, and that I'm a stranger. Whoever you want me to be."

"Okay." Mmm, yes-s-s, Gerard would be Veronique's after all. *Excellente*.

She heard him walk away, kept her eyes shut, her fingers eager now to get to work. A minute went by. Two. During which time she unfortunately had trouble focusing on Gerard because she couldn't help listening for Tyler.

Another minute. Another. She wasn't getting anywhere sexually and the anticipation made it harder to concentrate.

Then she heard his footsteps. Step. Step. Step.

Immediately her body responded and she had to slow her fingers to make the fantasy last.

Step. Step. Step. Darcy gave up on Gerard, gave up on the idea of a stranger. Tyler was coming, Tyler was nearly there with her.

Step. Step. Step.

She lifted her hips, breathing hard, having to force herself to go slowly and not rush this. Unlike last time, she felt totally safe, knowing Tyler would run interference on any other museum-goers.

Step. Step. Step.

A low breathy moan tried to leave her lips. She bit them together to keep it back.

Step. Step. Then she felt his body in the little room next to her chair. She pushed her hem up higher, higher, until she felt the room's air on her sex and knew he was able to see.

He whispered her name. A wave of even more intense excitement burst over her, shoving her nearly to the edge. Nearly…nearly…

Then other footsteps, coming closer. A lot of them. *Oh, no. No-no-no-no*. She quickened her pace, racing to come before anyone ruined her beautiful moment, but the anxiety this time was too much, pushing her arousal down too low to slide effortlessly over the brink.

Darn it.

She opened her eyes, brought her legs together, shoved to sit upright and yanked the hem of her skirt back down over her thighs. Darn, darn, darn and *damn* for good measure.

Tyler knelt next to her left thigh, hand on the arm of her chair, his body blocking her from the trio that had just walked in, looked curiously toward Darcy and Tyler, and started examining the sculpture and oohing and aahing over the view of the lake.

Darcy rolled her eyes. That is…she started to roll her eyes. As soon as she began to communicate her frustration, Tyler's hand began a little communication of its own, letting her know in no uncertain terms as it traveled up her inner thigh that the party wasn't over yet.

She pressed her legs together, shook her head, glanced at the three people, two older ladies and a man out for an evening of artistic appreciation.

They weren't watching. Tyler's hand pushed insistently, her skirt covering his forearm, his body still blocking her from view of the intruders. Desire ran too hot to resist. Surrender was her only option.

She met Tyler's darkened eyes, then slowly, deliberately loosened her thighs to give him access, hissing a tiny breath when his fingers made it to heaven.

"Now relax," he said quietly. "Forget they're here. Or if it turns you on more, don't forget."

She dared a look over at the elderly trio, still watching the lake, making comments about sailboats and whatever else they saw.

They had no idea.

She looked back at Tyler, thinking she had to be the luckiest woman in the world to meet someone who accepted so calmly her need to experiment with her fantasies.

"Let go. Let it come." He moved closer so he could whisper. "When I was standing watching you touch yourself I almost went out of my mind. I'm nearly out of it now, being able to feel you like this around my fingers."

She took a stuttering breath, feeling as if her insides were being painted with melted butter, which kept getting warmer and warmer with every stroke. Tyler kept up his rhythm, gaze unwavering. She darted more glances at the trio, but kept returning to him, to his deep watchful eyes and the tantalizing touch of his skilled fingers, sometimes rubbing, sometimes slipping inside her, always making her climb higher and higher.

"I'd like to bend you over this chair right now, in front of these people."

His low whisper made her wild. She stifled a gasp. Felt a light sheen of perspiration cover her skin as it always did when she got close to coming.

"I'd like to grab your hips and make you scream when you come, so loudly that security comes running and people panic. I'd like to have you contracting around my cock so hard that I can't help joining you."

A whimper escaped her. She grabbed his arm, clenched her jaw, nearly losing control, not caring that one quick look by any of the three other people in the room could get them in serious trouble.

"I want to come inside you so hard you can feel it."

She lifted her hips and came fast and violently, rigid in the chair, color flooding her face, strange snakelike sounds coming from between her teeth as she tried to hold back cries.

"Darcy—"

"Oh, no, you poor dear. Are you okay? Is she okay?"

Argh. Darcy's orgasm wound down too quickly, but the best

part had already happened and the aftershocks continued, deliciously unaffected by the unwelcome attention.

"She's fine. Fine." Tyler discreetly removed his hand from between her legs and turned to grin at the concerned trio. "Small seizure. It happens. Luckily she gets plenty of warning, so she was able to sit here where she could be safe when it…climaxed."

Darcy clenched her teeth harder. Laughter was trying so hard to exit her body that they undoubtedly thought her seizure had come back double.

"You poor thing. Should we get help?" The ladies looked on in fascinated horror.

"No. No. She's just coming…out of it now. Aren't you, sweetheart?"

She clamped down a giggle as hard as she could. "Yes. That was a *huge* one. But as soon as I recover I'll be ready to go again."

"If you're sure…" The trio moved out of the space, murmuring amongst themselves.

"Whew." Tyler chuckled and leaned in to kiss Darcy with passion that started her hormone machine humming again. When he stood, the bulge in his pants looked downright painful.

"Mmm." She stared pointedly. "Need any help with that?"

"I do." He pulled her to her feet, pressed her body against his. "But not here."

"Where?"

"How about in the middle of Cathedral Square Park? Elsa's should be jammed at this hour, we can put on a show." He winked and started out of the room, holding her hand. "I could do you over a bench or something, whadya think?"

"Ooh, baby."

"Just call me Mr. Romance."

She giggled and allowed herself to be pulled along faster than she would have walked otherwise. Apparently, Tyler was in a hurry. That suited her fine, even when he took the flights of stairs down at such speed that she practically had to leap three steps at a time to keep up. Damn shame they had two cars because she had something in mind for his ride that would probably cause an accident. When they got home, she'd make it all up to him.

In the meantime, she might as well admit the truth. She wasn't cut out for fantasies-come-true. Or putting it another way, which surprised and scared her a little: Tyler was her fantasy come true. What she was going to do about that, she still didn't know.

But she had a feeling the variations of this particular fantasy, who was right now pulling her along at sprinter speed, would keep her very happy and *very* satisfied for a long, long time.

Which meant she needed to make absolutely sure that her trip would be one hundred percent worth the pain of losing him.

13

TYLER WOKE TO SUN peeking under the shades in his room and a warm female curled up to his back. This was the way life was supposed to be. He closed his eyes again, peaceful and content beyond anything he could remember, listening tenderly to the soft regular breathing behind him.

He wanted to wake up to Darcy today and tomorrow and every morning for the rest of his life; there was no longer any question in his mind. He'd gone to the museum yesterday, heart like a boulder in his chest, ready to rescue Darcy from arrest or humiliation or whatever Molly was so sure she was facing, and then let her go. It had taken everything he had to act casual and natural around her, trying not to let his agony show.

Until she let slip that her self-pleasuring adventure hadn't gotten off the ground, and she wasn't sure why not. Then he'd dared to hope. And when her pleasure with him had not only gotten off the ground but flown a couple of times around the planet, he'd done more than hope. He'd become determined.

She had to understand now. After her first seduction fantasy, which succeeded beyond his, and he hoped, her wildest dreams, her second failed fantasy at Starlight and her strike-three fantasy at the museum, she had to see the big sign with both their names on it pointing the way to eternity.

Back at his house after the art museum last night, their sexual adventures had continued well into the wee hours until they both fell asleep from exhaustion, if nothing else. He'd be lucky if he could produce another sperm anytime this year. Between orgasms, they'd indulged in long conversations and a lot of laughter until the mood hit them both again, which it invariably seemed to do, each time sooner than he would have thought possible.

Did she think the endless excitement and pleasure they took in each other came only from hormonal activity? He'd experienced powerful, obsessive lust for women before, become intimate with some, and though he didn't have one-tenth Cam's experience, even he knew a perfect match like this was rare.

This morning after Darcy woke up, they had to talk this out. Now that he was so sure of his own feelings, he couldn't go on without a better understanding of where her head was, how she felt about her trip, about her life goals and about him. Whether she was as aware of the obvious as he was, or whether it would take more time to shatter her emotional denial and overcome stubborn resistance to change.

The problem of course was that they were nearly out of time. The balance had to tip one way or the other, toward her trip or toward her staying here. Or best of all, a compromise they could both live with. The only thing he wouldn't accept was that they couldn't at least hope for a future together.

Darcy stirred at his back and made a soft sound that turned his heart more vulnerable than it was already. He loved her. Wildly, unconditionally and completely. Everything about her, even the flaws he knew would drive him crazy and the ones he'd discover later that would drive him even more crazy. Bring it all on. Tyler was ready.

He just needed to know if she was.

She yawned and moved away on his queen-size bed to stretch. Too far away. He turned and laid his hand on her stomach, gazing at her face. Even with bed-head, puffy eyes and without makeup, she was the most beautiful thing he'd ever seen and he couldn't stand not to touch her.

Did he have it bad, or what?

"Good morning, Darcy Wolf."

"G'morning. Time's it?"

"Why? You have somewhere to be?" By sheer determination he kept his voice light. If she bolted now after she promised…

She shook her head and blinked sleepily. "Just curious."

Thank you, God. "It's about nine."

Darcy squinted at him. "Don't you have to get up and paint?"

"I'm taking the day off to help my parents. They have some old windows to haul to the drop-off center and Dad wants help fixing a leak in their basement."

"Good son." She put her hand to his cheek, then let it fall as if even that was too much effort. "Man. Tyler, I know this is weird, but I feel like someone had sex with me about forty times last night in about fifty different positions."

"Wow." He frowned concern and touched his palm to her forehead. "That sounds serious. I hope you're not coming down with something."

"Coitus uninterruptis?"

"Very possible."

"Hmm." She arranged her head higher on the pillow. "Sounds serious…ly fun. Is it contagious?"

"Hopelessly. But only when you're with the right person." He kissed a beautiful freckle on her gorgeous naked shoulder. "Ready for more?"

"Mmm, I need a week to recover."

He froze, lips only a few inches from her skin. "We don't have much more than that, Darcy."

The charged silence forced him to move. He lifted his head to find her contented smile had vanished.

So. Now was the right moment. Except he had no idea how

to begin. *Do you love me?* was what he really wanted to know, but no self-respecting man would ever ask that.

"You're still planning to go."

"I...am."

At least she hesitated. "No change of heart, huh?"

"Big change of heart." Her fingers stroked a path from his shoulder to his elbow. "No change of plans, though. At least...well, I guess I've been having too much fun to really think about it."

"Ah." That hurt. He'd rather she'd done nothing but agonize over how much it would pain her to be without him. "So what's the plan now? You move to Seattle and then what? Get a job?"

"Mostly I'll take classes and volunteer. Maybe in a few schools or hospitals, believe it or not. I helped tutor kids at Children's Hospital when I was in high school." Her smile was wry. "You'd think I'd have had enough of sick people."

"You love kids." He squeezed her hand. "I'm glad. I want kids someday, too."

Her gaze turned cautious and she made a noncommittal sound, a combination "oh" and "mmm," like a yoga mantra.

He'd pushed too far. "When you get back in eight years, what do you plan to do?"

She frowned and irritably pushed hair out of her face. "I don't know that I'll want to come back here."

Ouch. His turn for the yoga mantra. "Oh-mmm."

"I'd still like to go back to school to get my master's in educational psychology."

"What about marriage and kids?"

"I want those, too."

"After the degree? Before? During?"

"I don't..."

"If you meet someone in Seattle, will you skip Los Angeles?

If you hate Los Angeles, will you go directly to Miami? If you pass go, will you collect two hundred dollars?"

"Stop." She rose onto her elbow, laughing, and swatted his shoulder. "I don't want to think about this now. A lot can happen. I hope a lot does happen. Some of which might determine how and where I end up at age thirty-four. I don't want to plan it now."

"Eight years, Darcy." His voice came out husky and low. "I don't want to lose you for that long."

She swallowed. "I wouldn't expect you to wait."

"How about a compromise? Six months in each city. Or six weeks." He poked her arm teasingly. "Six hours?"

"I don't know." She pursed her lips. "Two years seemed like the minimum to feel less like a tourist and more like a native."

He couldn't stand it. She was talking too easily about being gone for that long, not nearly enough as if it would rip her heart out to be away from him. Not that he'd ever wish pain on her, but... "I'm betting you don't end up feeling native anywhere but here."

"That's what Molly says." She let herself fall back on the bed and stared glumly at his ceiling fan, which paradoxically brightened his mood.

"Maybe she's right."

"Maybe." She shifted her gaze to him. "It's a lot to ask that I change my life plan for you after knowing you such a short time."

"I don't want you to change it for me." He lay back down next to her, followed the smooth contour of her cheekbone with his finger. "I want you to change it for you."

"But when I'm going on this trip for me in the first place..." She took hold of his wrist, pressed his palm to her cheek. "You told me you made yourself be grown-up and sensible after Cam died. You have to understand what it's like to want to bust out and take risks for a change."

"Isn't committing to someone you feel a lot for but don't know that well a bigger risk than taking a trip?"

"I'm not talking about that kind of risk. I mean a real challenge to what you've always thought about yourself and about your life."

"Staying would be exactly that. A challenge to the idea that you can't be anyone but who you've always been here."

A furrow rushed to occupy the space between her eyebrows. Good. He was making her think. "If you and I are supposed to work out, a few years apart shouldn't matter."

"A few? Eight isn't a few. Eight is nearly a decade."

"I know. It's…a long time." She let go of his hand, sat up restlessly, hugged her knees under the sheet. "I do understand that you want me to stay, but…"

"I gave that away, really? And here I thought I was being so subtle."

She laughed. "More subtle than Molly, but that's not saying much."

"No. But…" He pushed himself up to sit next to her, pressing his shoulder to hers. "I have a higher stake in you staying here than Molly."

"Oh?" She smiled and nudged him. "What's that?"

"I love you." The words came out unexpectedly, but they couldn't have been truer and he didn't regret them. "I love you and if you leave it's going to tear me apart."

She started. Stared. Tears began rolling from her wide blue-gray eyes down her suddenly pale cheeks. "Oh, Tyler. I've only known you a couple of weeks. How can you be so sure so soon?"

"Love at first sight." He grinned, wishing Katie could hear him. She wouldn't stop laughing for a month.

"What's so funny?"

"My sister married a man a few days after she met him. I went off the deep end and accused her of making the worst, most foolish and irresponsible mistake of her life, one that made Cam's tricks look amateur. That was two years ago. Until recently we barely spoke."

"So…what happened recently?" She looked a little frightened, as if she already knew the answer.

"I met you and realized it was possible to fall head-over-heels in love with someone when you're painting her house and she walks outside and looks up at you with her hand across her forehead like a visor, and you touch your cap automatically to say 'nice to meet you,' then make eye contact and, boom, practically fall off the ladder.

"So you paint slowly and hang around after the rest of the crew leaves, just to talk to her. And talking to her makes you so nervous you can barely get any words out, and at the same time you have this incredible comfortable sensation of knowing her already.

"And when she sits in the yard in a bikini, you nearly break the window over and over because you're so damn distracted. And later, when you see her taking her clothes off through that same glass just for you, and you make love to her and go places in your mind, heart and body you've never been before, you realize…" He shrugged. "You realize that just because something hasn't happened to you yet doesn't mean it can't happen at all."

"Tyler…" She seemed unable to say more.

"After I met you I called my sister, got down on my knees, figuratively, and apologized because I knew she was right." He picked up her hand, kissed her fingers and held them against his lips. "I fell in love with you the second I saw you."

She turned away, appeared to be making a careful study of the wall opposite his bed. "You're making this more complicated than it already is. I've lived nothing but complicated for the last decade plus. I thought life would finally be simple for a change."

"What can we do? We can't un-meet each other." He put his arm around her. "I'm not doing this to torture you, you know."

"I know." She sounded miserable and he could barely stand it.

"The complications come only from fighting what you feel."

"I guess. Maybe." She twisted her mouth pensively. "I didn't believe in love at first sight, either."

"And…now?" He couldn't believe his voice came out at all when his heart's chance to keep beating seemed to be riding on her answer.

"Now I'm not so sure."

His heart kept right on beating. Faster and harder as if it were running a race. His lips stretched into a grin. All the answer he needed. She was his. Only a matter of time. Just a matter of finding whatever it was that would tip her over onto his side. "Tell you what."

"What?" She looked so apprehensive he had to keep himself from chuckling. Amazing how he could feel so many emotions for one person. Animal lust, tenderness so deep and sweet he could hardly stand it, plus alternating bouts of joy and certainty, and fear and frustration. No wonder, as his sister said, writers found the emotion such an endless source for their creativity.

"For the next week we'll do this your way. Let the topic rest, have fun and not worry about what's going to happen. Okay?"

"Okay. Yes." She smiled her relief.

"On one condition."

Wary, wary eyes. "What's that?"

"You think about how you feel about me, how you feel about us, and why and what you're really leaving behind. Think whether it's possible if you feel the same way about me as I do about you, that the only complication is you not letting life happen the way it's supposed to."

"You believe in fate."

"I believe I feel this way about you for a reason, and ignoring that reason amounts to a lifetime of missing out on something really special."

She nodded, tried to smile, but any idiot could see the confusion in her eyes. He hated to be that idiot. He wanted to be the one making that smile real. But if offering love couldn't get her to change her mind...

His sister's words came back to him. *If you don't ask, Shoelace, you won't be giving her enough to stay for.*

Maybe Katie was right. If he wanted Darcy to understand exactly how serious he was about her staying...maybe he should buy a ring and ask her to marry him.

DARCY DRAGGED HERSELF down Clarke Avenue toward Roosevelt Elementary School, still twelve long blocks away. Her body had seen plenty of exercise the night before, ahem, and her hips protested every step, but she couldn't stand another second in her almost-empty house. She had nothing to shop for since she wanted to pack light for her trip, and most of her friends were at work so she couldn't pester them for company to distract her from her confusion. Molly had plenty on her plate right now and would only tell Darcy again how she was a fool for leaving now that she'd found Tyler. Especially now that she knew Tyler loved her.

A shot of adrenaline increased her pace for the next half block. Love! So soon. The story about him making up with his sister nearly had Darcy in tears. He'd spoken evenly, but she could tell the sibling split had weighed heavily.

He loved her. And she...almost was sort of sure she did, too. Kind of. Help.

But not sure enough to cancel her trip. What if the New Her she evolved into away from Milwaukee wasn't right for Tyler, and there was someone out there who'd fit a truer version of herself?

The source of all this angst had fed her breakfast this morning—damn, the man could cook—and then made such sweet beautiful love to her on the couch in his living room, because they couldn't make it upstairs, that she thought she'd die if she ever had to leave him.

And yet…she'd die if she stayed here. Same place, same friends, same stores, same schools, same same same. Not to mention that once her house was sold, where would she live? What would she do? Pursuing her master's would certainly be worthwhile, but it was too late to attend this fall. What then? The same volunteer work she planned to do in Seattle? It held no appeal locally. Always been here, already done that.

She wanted to explore what was between her and Tyler, yes. No question. But he was going to have a tremendous amount to accomplish when he started teaching and would be extremely busy this next year. Plus, if she stayed for him, she'd be tied here again, changing her life for yet another man, worse now for having finally earned her freedom and come so close to being able to capitalize on it.

Horrible to be caught between the proverbial rock and the hard place. Her planned trip rocked, but she adored Tyler's hard place.

Even that bad joke couldn't make her smile. She passed Center Street Park and her feet took her up the diagonal path to the wood-chip-covered playground currently being enjoyed on this cloudy mild day by preschool kids and their attentive moms and dads. Without deciding to, she continued over to the swing set and clambered aboard one of the swings, because why not?

Up… Down… Back… Forth… A perfect visual aid for the dilemma she was facing. Stay… Go… Stay… Go…

Up. Stay here and suffocate from claustrophobia.

Down. Go and die of loneliness without Tyler.

Stay… Go… Back… Forth—

Her cell phone rang. She slowed her speed and hauled it out of her pocket, squinted at the display. "Hi-lo, Molly."

"He-e-ey there!"

A definite improvement in her tone. "You sound cheerful. What's up?"

"What's up? Bruce was. Last night. Twice. Or three times, I lost count."

"Whoa." Darcy made a face of silly astonishment, which in turn made a darling dark-eyed little boy staring at her take his hand out of his mouth to point and laugh. Much to the embarrassment of his mother. "What happened to Bruce?"

"Fun-ny wady."

"Super Nightie happened. Oh, it was sooo good." Molly practically sang the words. "I feel *quite* delightful today."

"Uh-huh. So what, you called just to tell me you got—" she blinked at the little boy, in earshot, especially when she swung closer "—some?"

"Shum?" The little boy looked way too curious.

"And…best of all—" Molly giggled girlishly, which was so not Molly "—you were right. The personal trainer aka Angelina Jolie look-alike is a big major nada."

"Ha!" Darcy was so happy for her friend she pumped her non-phone-carrying fist in the air, which nearly made her fall off the seat. Her frantic grab for the chain cracked the little boy up so hard, drool ran down his fingers, which had been firmly planted back in his mouth. "I knew it! I told you. Oh, Molly, I'm so happy."

"Hap-pee?"

"I was such an idiot. You knew I was. How could I not have trusted my Bruce? Except I did trust him, I just thought he was getting in over his head with Lo-lee-tah."

"And he wasn't."

"No! Get this. He thought I was pulling away because he'd

gained so much weight." Her voice thickened with emotion. "He was trying to lose the pounds for *me*. So I'd think he was sexy again. As if I ever stopped! I probably pulled away first because I was tired or stressed out by life in general, probably when that fund-raiser came to a head at Annabel's school, and then he reacted to me pulling away by pulling away and then I reacted to him pulling away by pulling away more, and then…well, you know the rest."

"Wow. That is really romantic. I mean for Bruce to actually *exercise*."

"Et-so-sighs?" The boy started flapping his elbows as if he were doing the chicken dance.

"I know. I know! I'm so happy. It's like we fell in love all over again. He's groping me in the kitchen when the kids aren't looking, playing footsie with me during breakfast. It's amazing. I'm so happy."

"Me, too, Moll. That's fabulous."

"Fa-boo-wuss."

"He's taking me out to dinner at Bartalotta's Steak House tomorrow! We're getting a sitter so we can take our time."

"Oh, now that is really—"

"And! The best part? We're going to start trying for another baby."

Darcy put on the expected squeal, making the little boy laugh again. "A baby. Oh, my gosh."

"Oh-dosh."

She pictured Molly swelling, glowing, Bruce at her side, loving and protective, Annabel and Kyle looking on proudly. The swing fell lower. The mom tugged her little boy's free hand and he stumbled away, glancing back over his shoulder once in a while at Darcy until his mother distracted him with a ride on a little car attached to the top of a giant spring.

What would it be like to have life inside you? Darcy thought of herself and Tyler and a little boy, fist in his mouth, eyes big and dark enough to melt both their hearts with a look. A child that contained such a big part of each of them.

"We'd always said two kids, and apparently he thought I didn't want another and I thought he didn't and—" She broke off and laughed breathlessly. "I love this man. He makes me so happy. I love his guts, every part of him."

"That's sooo wonderful." The swing slowed further. Her foot brushed the ground and jerked her sideways.

"I can't imagine how I got this lucky."

"You totally deserve it." Darcy stopped the swing, feet planted in the wood chips, feeling hollow and strange. Not as happy as she should be for her friend. Not nearly as happy.

Oh, God. Here she was about to spit on the most wonderful man she'd ever met by running off for fabulous adventures she might or might not have. A man who said he loved her and wanted her to stay. And no matter how much she told herself she'd always regret not going, always wonder what could have been if she followed her dream, there was nothing she could do about the growing part of her that desperately, desperately wanted what Molly had with Bruce, which she might be able to have with Tyler.

She slipped off the swing. "I couldn't be happier for you."

"So *I* stopped being an idiot, when are *you* going to?"

"I'm sorry?"

"How's the progress on admitting you don't really want to go on this crazy trip when true love has plans for you here?"

Darcy let out a growl of frustration that made a little girl coming down the slide panic and try to stop herself from getting any closer to the nasty wild lady.

"Sorry." Darcy smiled apologetically at the girl's mother, arms out ready to catch her child.

"Why sorry?"

"No, not you." She headed for the sidewalk to get back to her sore-hipped constitutional. "Listen, I don't need your lectures. I already got worked over by Tyler this morning."

"Ah, good man. I should call him so we can discuss a battle strategy."

Darcy snorted. "Well, *that* should be familiar. I'm sure his number is in your speed dial labeled 'stop Darcy's idiocy.'"

"Oh." Molly laughed nervously. "So, uh, you kind of figured that one out, huh?"

"Who else knew I was at Starlight and the art museum? Where Tyler not coincidentally showed up each time?"

"Okay, so I meddled a little."

"A lot, Molly."

"A lot. But it was good, wasn't it?"

Darcy sighed and stopped to stretch a tight calf muscle. What *had* they been doing last night? "On principle, no. As it turned out…okay, yes."

"So by now you should trust me in all things, my dear. And if I say you need to give up this trip and grab that man by the——"

"I know. I know."

"And?"

"And I'll think about it."

"Promise?"

"Yes! Get off the phone. You're making me insane."

"Okay, okay."

Darcy grinned and resumed her walk. If she left, she'd miss Molly like mad, too. "I'm really happy for you, Moll."

"Me, too. Thanks, sweetie."

Darcy hung up the phone, more confused than she'd ever been, which ten minutes ago she would have sworn wasn't possible. It was so much easier to sneer at coupledom when Molly and Bruce were driving each other crazy. But the radiant happiness beaming through Darcy's phone from her best friend resonated only too well with the joy Darcy felt around Tyler.

She was crazy about him. No, she loved him. Maybe Molly was right and Darcy should just get over herself and admit it to the world.

14

TYLER PULLED INTO a parking lot opposite Ingram's Jewelry store, where his father and grandfather had bought engagement rings for their wives. He'd shopped for a ring for Annie, but panicked and never bought one, even though he'd been more sure of Annie than he was of Darcy. At the time he'd told himself she'd want to pick out her own. Now he wondered if deep down he knew they weren't meant to be. Which made his errand today a sign of his instinct being on board with his intentions this time.

He wouldn't lie and say he wasn't anxious. Nor was he the only one who was. When he hinted to his parents that he'd met someone he was serious about, they seemed delighted and launched into the expected questions. Delighted until they found out how long he'd known her and that he was thinking marriage. Then came the exchanged glances and the worry lines on his mother's forehead.

Obviously they were thinking about the last time he'd asked a woman for the rest of her life. He'd been so sure Annie would say yes, that when she said, "Oh, no, Tyler! You shouldn't have done this," he'd grinned away, the beaming groom-to-be, until the "no" part of her reaction, and the fact that she meant he *really* shouldn't have, made it into his brain.

He turned the car off and emerged into the sunshine. Enough negative thinking. He was sure enough that he and Darcy belonged together that he was ready to invest in the symbol of their commitment. The pain of Annie's refusal turned out to be one hundred percent worth it, since it ensured he was free now to be with Darcy. If Annie had accepted, he couldn't imagine how he'd have reacted when sideswiped by this overwhelming passion for another woman.

A bell tinkled as he pulled open the door to Ingram's. His anxiety increased. A glance at the window display had shown mostly necklaces, very few rings. Inside, on a rather nauseating shade of green carpet, stood glass counters and display cases with jewelry and fine watches.

"May I help you find something?" A young blond woman whose name tag read "Cheryl" smiled questioningly.

"Hi, Cheryl. I'm Tyler." He cleared his throat. "I'm looking for a…ring."

"Engagement? Wedding? Friendship? Gradua—"

"Engagement." He could barely get the word out. Engaged. He'd be engaged. Wasn't that something that happened to other people?

"Wonderful. We have a beautiful assortment over here." She walked a few feet to her left and indicated the counter with a perfectly manicured hand, which, he noticed, sported a ring bearing a diamond the size of a cranberry. Did Darcy want one of those? He didn't see her as the cranberry-coveting type.

"What is her taste?"

He had no idea. "Oh. Well. Let me see what you have."

Rocks. Rocks and more rocks. So many rocks he felt dazzled staring at them all. Not necessarily in a good way. Perfect shiny diamonds on perfect round gold.

"This is a lovely one." She took out a three-stone ring that looked chunky to him. Did Darcy like that kind? "Or this one."

The second was simpler, one large diamond circled by many

tiny ones. To him it looked top-heavy. How the hell was he going to choose?

"Or this?" A diamond with a ruby on either side. Would Darcy need to wear red every day? He didn't think she wore the color often. Women cared about that stuff, didn't they?

"Or this one?" A twisted band, enormous rectangular stone. He had no clue what she'd think. He wasn't even sure what he thought.

Apparently he'd expected to find the perfect ring sitting on a velvet cushion in a blinding spotlight with a sign that said, Here, Tyler, Buy This One.

He was in way over his head.

"Can you hold on a second?" He beat a retreat near a case of watches and whipped out his cell phone, feeling like a completely inept example of a hopeful fiancé. "Molly. It's Tyler."

"Hey there, what's up?"

"Uh, I'm in a jewelry store…"

"Ye-e-e-s?"

"And I want to buy…something. For Darcy."

"A-a-a-nd?"

"So, I wondered if you knew what her taste was."

"I-i-i-n?"

Tyler rolled his eyes. He'd wanted to keep this between himself and Darcy, but there was no way. "Rings."

"What ki-i-ind?"

"Eng-a-a-gement."

A small gasp, then a shriek that nearly deafened him. "Oh my gosh, oh my gosh!"

"Molly…"

"When did you ask her? Is she there? No, of course she's not there. She would have called me herself. When are you asking her? Before she leaves? Of course before she leaves. Do you think she'll decide to stay? Oh, I know she will if you ask her to marry you, I know she will. This is so exciting! Did you tell me when you're asking her?"

"Have I been able to get one word in?"

"Uh…no. Sorry."

"I just want to know her taste."

"Her taste. Wow. Uh…she doesn't wear much jewelry, but the stuff she has is mostly small."

"Small." He frowned. He'd been right that the boulder diamonds weren't her style. But buying a pebble seemed cheap. Let's face it, if you sprang for a solitaire, all anyone looked at was the size. He wasn't into having his financial standing secretly rated every time someone offered his or her best wishes to the bride-to-be.

Darcy. His bride. A floaty sensation entered his head. Not quite dizziness but not comfortable, either.

"Which jewelers?"

"Ingram's."

"Oh, I love that store! Bruce bought my ring there."

He tried to imagine Molly's ring and came up empty. "Oh. Yeah, okay."

"Ask for the antique stuff. I bet she'd like that."

"Antique stuff. I will."

"You'll be all right?"

Tyler snorted. "Uh, yes, Molly, I'm a big boy now."

"Sorry. Have fun. I don't know how I'm going to keep this from Darcy, but I promise I will."

"That would definitely be appreciated."

"Can I call Bruce?"

He sighed. Might as well say yes. She'd do it anyway. "Sure."

"Oh, goody! He'll be thrilled and so am I, Tyler! I had a feeling about you two. Good luck finding the perfect ring. If Ingram's doesn't have anything, you can try—"

"Molly. I'll manage."

"Right, sorry. Butting out."

He thanked her for her help and hung up the phone, strode back over to the lovely Cheryl, feeling slightly more confident. "She'd like an antique ring."

"The antique engagement rings are here." She indicated a smaller section of the counter, which still had way too many options. "See anything you like?"

He studied the selection, confidence sagging again. Many beautiful rings. Many. Ornate, less ornate, too many stones, not enough stones, too fussy, too staid. Nothing that leaped out and shouted "Darcy." This was not going to be easy. Cheryl waited expectantly. Total silence in the shop. He started to sweat.

"Let me look at that one." He pointed to one that looked pretty enough.

"Ah, yes. This is a replica 1930's Art Deco ring." She inserted a key, slid back the cabinet door and plucked out the ring. "The center diamond is princess cut, a little over one carat. As you can see, the white-gold band has beautiful vine-like designs all the way around the band, ten additional channel set diamonds, five on either side, and two secret diamonds on the sides below the main stone."

"Mmm-hmm." The ring was gorgeous, no question. But was it Darcy? He tried to picture this formal, elegant piece of jewelry on her finger and couldn't. The ring seemed too perfect, too unapproachable. Not enough like Darcy. "Do you have anything more…friendly?"

"Friendly?" She spoke gently. *Poor man, such a shame about the brain damage.* "Do you mean…in a lower price range?"

"No." He rubbed the back of his neck. She probably thought he should be buying his ring at Wal-Mart with *Have a Super Day* spelled out in cubic zirconium. "It's not the price. This one just…"

The bell tinkled by the front door. Another customer. Maybe Cheryl would wait on whoever it was and leave him alone with his silly desire for a friendly ring.

"Tyler, my man! What's this I hear about you signing up for the ball-and-chain club?"

Oh, no. Bruce. He turned, still leaning on the counter. "Molly sent you."

"No, no, no. I was in the area, thought I'd…" He saw Tyler's skeptical scowl and nodded sheepishly. "She thought you might need some help. You know how she is."

Tyler shook his head and smiled. "You look great, Bruce."

"Twenty pounds gone, going for thirty more." Bruce patted his once-enormous belly. "Hey, that is one gorgeous ring you got there."

"Yeah…" Tyler turned back to the newly hopeful Cheryl.

"Let's see what else we got." Bruce leaned his six-foot-three body over and carefully scanned the other rings under the counter, glancing now and then at the one Tyler had picked out. Cheryl was undoubtedly holding her breath.

Finally, Bruce straightened and pointed. "You don't need me. That's the best of the bunch, right there in your hand."

"I don't know."

Cheryl's smile slipped.

Bruce winked at her and slapped Tyler on the back, nearly making him drop the ring. "Trust me, I totally understand what you're feeling right now. It doesn't quite seem real, does it?"

"No." Not remotely.

"One thing to decide in your own head to get married, another to come to a place like this and have to make the decision concrete. I felt exactly the same way when I came here for Molly's ring."

Tyler frowned at the sparkling diamonds between his fingers. Was that all it was? A natural and typical episode of cold feet? He'd out-and-out panicked while ring shopping for Annie. At least this fear wasn't that bad.

"You're not going to find a prettier ring than that one. It's a beauty."

Cheryl beamed at Bruce. Tyler had the impression she'd have hugged him if she could.

"Good morning." An older man emerged from the back of the store and shuffled over to join Tyler's impromptu ring-shopping party.

"Mr. Ingram, good morning." Bruce saluted him with a brief wave. "How's business?"

"Not bad, not bad." He clearly had no idea who Bruce was, but his eyes lit up when he saw what Tyler had in his hand. "I see you've got the 1930's replica. Beautiful ring. Don't design them like that anymore. That one's my personal favorite."

Uh-huh. And when the next customer came in, whatever ring he chose would be Mr. Ingram's new personal favorite.

"See?" Bruce held his hands up as if nothing could be more obvious. "This is the one."

Tyler nodded slowly. The ring was beautiful. Darcy couldn't help but love it. Excitement started burning in his stomach. Or was that acid indigestion? He took a deep breath, feeling as if there wasn't enough air in the shop. He'd taken a leap of faith deciding to trust his feelings for Darcy. Why not take this one, too? "Yeah. Okay. I'll take it."

"Atta boy." Bruce stuck out his hand and Tyler shook uneasily. "Congratulations, man. She's a terrific woman."

Tyler unclenched his jaw. Couldn't they turn on the air-conditioning in here? It felt like August. "She sure is."

"Do you know her size?"

Tyler turned blankly toward Cheryl. Her size? "She's pretty slender. Six? Eight?"

Bruce cracked up.

Cheryl hid a smile. "Her *ring* size."

"Oh." He shook his head, feeling vaguely panicky. "No. I don't, sorry."

"This is a six and a half. But if it doesn't fit, she can bring it back and we'll size it for her, okay?"

"Sure. Yes. Okay." He managed a grin, but it didn't come naturally. Maybe he was just having a flashback to the pain he'd felt when Annie refused him. Or maybe his subconscious was telling him that regarding leaps of faith, he'd leaped plenty already.

Cheryl went over to the register and started fussing with papers and forms and boxes. Tyler drifted toward another counter, wiping his forehead, feeling as if his collar and tie were too tight. Except he was wearing a T-shirt.

This was the right thing to do, wasn't it? He gripped the edge of the counter and glanced down through the glass.

There it was.

The ring. A slender, silver-colored band—white-gold? platinum?—twisted just once on either side of a small perfect circle-cut diamond. Under and around the diamond, in contrast to the graceful curving lines, a small square of yellow-gold was set diagonally, its sharp angles framing and enhancing the round stone and the arching metal.

It was perfect.

"Wait." He whirled around, holding his hands up like a traffic cop. "Stop."

Cheryl froze, fingers poised over the register buttons, face showing horror. "Those are *friendship* rings over there, sir."

"I don't care." He jabbed repeatedly on the glass, breathing deep gulps of the now-plentiful fresh air, pure joy—definitely not acid this time—churning through his system. Hot damn. He was going to get married.

"This is it. This is Darcy's ring."

15

"YOU'LL KNOCK HIM DEAD." Molly beamed at Darcy from where she sprawled on the king-size bed in Bruce's and her bedroom.

Darcy frowned at herself in the full-length mirror on Molly's closet door. Her friend had insisted she borrow a timeless little black dress from among Molly's "skinny clothes." "You're sure this isn't too dressy? We're just eating at his place."

"I'm sure, I'm sure. Why do you keep asking?"

"Because it seems too—"

"Tomorrow night is your farewell party here, the next night we're all going out after we help move the last of your stuff, the morning after that you're leaving. When are you going to see him alone again after tonight? Shouldn't your last evening together be special?"

Darcy scowled to hide the fact that her lip wanted to quiver and she wanted to start bawling. She loathed phrases like "last night together," since they always threatened to set her off. To be honest, whether she told herself she was going or told herself she was staying, neither felt real. She had made peace with how deeply she felt about Tyler. Especially after the past week together—light and fun, exactly as Tyler had promised—during which they'd found more thrills in good old Milwaukee than she ever thought possible. Not that he showed her any new places or gave her new insights, but the lakefront was so much more fun when they could huddle under a blanket enjoying the view and surreptitiously get each other off underneath. And the Dome's greenhouse buildings were much more scenic when she got kissed under the cacao tree and fondled near the cactus. Likewise she'd never forget another nighttime tumble in his van, this time parked at Robert's Custard, after rich Rocky Road frozen custard dripped down her cleavage and Tyler went after it with his tongue. Nor would her alma mater ever evoke the same memories after her private orgasmic tour of what would be his office space.

Obviously there was a lot more to discover about Milwaukee and Tosa than she'd ever dreamed. But also more to discover about herself. The woman who could cut loose that way—Darcy wanted to explore her, that wild part of herself that had been suppressed for so long, before she settled down with anyone.

"Trust me." Molly set her chin on her hands. "You look perfect for tonight."

"If you say so." Darcy smoothed the clingy skirt, adjusted the tiny straps and admired the nearly off-shoulder neckline.

"If nothing else, think of it as inspiration for me. Bruce has got me going with him to see Lolita."

"Really? You're working out together?"

"I want to be in shape for this baby." She nodded emphatically toward Darcy's outfit. "And I want to be able to wear that dress again even if pregnancy happens."

"That is an honorable goal." Darcy turned to view the low scooped back of the bodice. "You're sure I don't look too—"

"*Oy vey,* woman. Stop kvetching. You look edible and he's goink to vant to devour you. I would not steer you wronk in dis, dahlink."

Darcy giggled at Molly's impersonation of her German-Jewish mother. "Okay, okay. I'll wear it."

"You won't regret it. I promise."

"I'll hold you to that." She turned away from the mirror and stepped into the too-high heels Molly had ordered her to bring to go with the dress. "Tyler sounded odd this afternoon."

Molly lifted her chin off her hands. "Odd how?"

"I don't know. A little manic or something."

"He's cooking a special dinner for the woman he loves. What's not to be manic about?"

"But he said it's mostly finger food, not a sit-down formal meal. Most of it was make-ahead. I don't know." She frowned, then winced as she took a step. "Did the Marquis de Sade invent dress shoes for women?"

"Undoubtedly, yes. Don't worry about Tyler. He's probably dreading this trip, *which you will soon decide you're not really taking*, and is trying to sound cheerful so you don't feel guilty."

Darcy sighed. Molly refused to acknowledge even the possibility of her adventure. That Darcy hadn't yet decided a hundred percent whether she was going or not drove Molly nearly as crazy as it drove Darcy. "If I'm not going, why are you still throwing me a party?"

"Why not? Parties are fun. We can celebrate some other occasion instead."

"I guess." Darcy glanced at her watch. "I better go. You're sure I look okay?"

"Argh. Get. Out." Molly flung out a plump arm to point to the door. "Go. I'm going to strangle you if you ask me again."

"Right. Going. Thanks for the dress. It's just perfect—how did you know?" She grinned at Molly's exasperation and went carefully down the steep stairs to the first floor, where she was treated to a long wolf whistle.

"Hey, look at you! Tyler's a lucky man."

"Hi, Bruce. Your wife did this to me. That makes *you* the lucky man."

"You know it." He walked her to the back door and held it open. "Have fun tonight. Tell Tyler I said to give me a ring later."

"I will. Good night." She waved, wondering what he thought was so funny about Tyler giving him a call, and walked gingerly out to her car. These shoes would not last long. She'd only worn them once and had conveniently forgotten the pain aspect. Luckily she rarely stayed in clothes more than a few minutes around Tyler.

Her throat constricted as she got in the car and pulled out of the driveway, heading north. Molly and Bruce owned a relatively tiny place in Washington Highlands, the toniest area of Wauwatosa, some properties with garages the size of Darcy's whole house. But beautiful. Peaceful. Wisconsin.

She turned left on Two Tree Lane, immersed in wistful nostalgia. She'd moved to the house on 63rd Street when she was three years old…

Uh-huh. She roused herself. And had never been *anywhere else*.

She turned left on North, right on 64th, and drove the few blocks up to Tyler's bungalow on the right, with those silly lion statues standing sentry outside the front door. Tonight they looked noble, though, and a bit sad. Or was it just her mood?

Tyler opened the door in casual olive pants and an olive-and-navy patterned knit shirt he hadn't bothered tucking in. She was about to feel extremely stupid and told-you-so to Molly about her getup, when he looked her up and down and his eyes shot wide in comic appreciation. That changed her mind in a hurry. *Clearly* the dress was perfect. She owed Molly a big thank-you-very-much.

"Wow."

"I wasn't going to go formal, but Molly suggested it."

Something registered in his face that she didn't understand. "I'll bet she did. Tell me, is there anything in this city Molly doesn't control?"

Darcy pretended to think. "Nope. She should run for mayor."

"She doesn't have to. Come here. You look incredible." He met her at the threshold and planted a kiss on her neck, her cheek, then, mmm, on her lips. The faint aroma of something spicy and delicious clung to his clothing. "You've been hard at work?"

"Just heating something in the oven."

"Mmm, I like things hot."

"You certainly do." He pressed her body against his and kissed her lingeringly. "Come in or I'm going to end up making love to you here in the coat closet."

"And this would be bad how?" She slid her hands up the strong muscles of his back.

"I'm sure there's a reason."

"Can you think of it?" Her hips started a persuasive rhythm against his fly; she lifted her knee and he caught her thigh with one hand and ground more firmly against her.

"Um…appetizers will burn?"

"Darn." She leaned back, keeping her arms around him, feigning deep disappointment. "That's probably the only excuse I'll accept. Otherwise—"

"Take that inside!"

Darcy and Tyler turned abruptly to find Annika, lips pursed, eyes enormous with disapproval behind her huge glasses, her little Scottie Scotty staring at them, panting as if he wanted more of the passion show, not less.

Tyler sighed and let go of Darcy's leg. "Hi, Annika."

"Close the door on that pornography. This is a family street. Darcy Wolf, is that you?"

"Yes, it's me. Hello." Thank God her dad wasn't around to be driven crazy by any more of Annika's State-of-the-Block reports.

"If your father were still alive, young lady, I'd—"

"I'm sure you would. Bye, Annika." Tyler leaned toward Darcy with his mouth wide open and his tongue hanging out, as if he were going to give her the soggiest, most X-rated French kiss ever, while slowly swinging his front door shut so Annika would miss the best part.

Click. The latch caught closed and Darcy burst out laughing. "She'll be furious."

"She loved it." Tyler took her hand and led her toward the delicious smells in his kitchen, which was more spacious than hers, done in cream tile with hardwood flooring and walnut cabinets. Several dishes were laid out already on the small table, including colorful assorted roasted peppers sprinkled with cheese and vinaigrette dressing; a loaf of crusty bread; bowls of nuts, pickles and vegetables; a tomato, cheese and onion tart studded with black olives; a platter of sliced cured meats that looked Italian and some cheeses that looked French.

"Oh my gosh."

Tyler was taking what looked like herbed puff pastry rounds out of the oven. "I hope you're hungry."

"How could I not be? Everything looks incredible. And the smells, mmm."

"Good." He transferred the pastries to a rack. "Would you like some champagne?"

"I never ever say no to champagne."

"Or much else, I noticed."

She crossed to him and planted a smiling kiss on his lips. "I have a good idea. Why don't you transfer to the University of Seattle for two years, then UCLA for two, then U of Miami and finally, why not Harvard?"

"Sure, I'll get right on that." He was twisting the wire cage off a bottle of Pol Roger, which had been Darcy's mom's favorite special-occasion champagne according to Darcy's tee-totaling father. She still missed knowing Dad was around to worry about her, as much as his protectiveness annoyed her. She didn't think he'd approve of her recent, er, capers around town at all, though, or her seemingly self-indulgent travel plans, so maybe life had worked out the way destiny intended.

The cork came out with a deep, hollow pop and vapor curled up from the bottle's mouth along with the faint hiss of bubbles.

"Expertly done."

"Why, thank you." He poured into two crystal tulip glasses, sealed the champagne with a stopper, put it back in the refrigerator and handed her a glass.

"A toast." He clinked his champagne to hers. "Here's to new beginnings."

"New begin—" Darcy's voice caught and she had to clear her throat. How could she think of a new beginning if it meant an ending with this wonderful man?

She half wanted to call Molly to tell her to cancel the farewell party, due to lack of leaving. But only half.

"Let's go into the living room. If you take my champagne, please, I'll bring the tray of food."

"I'm on it." She followed him into his living room, a far cry from the shades-of-beige decor his great-aunt had before him.

"Too bad it's not cool enough to light a fire. That'll probably have to wait for fall."

Darcy stopped in the middle of the room, holding the quietly fizzing glasses. Fall. How could she miss fall? How could she miss curling up next to Tyler in this room with a crackling fire making shadows waver on the walls?

In winter, how could she miss cozy evenings watching snow-flakes float, drinking hot chocolate or brandy or coffee spiked with Bailey's while she studied and he corrected papers?

While she was at it, what about spring? A rebirth, a reawakening, the giddiness of warm weather returning, their first-year anniversary in May.

How could she miss any of it?

"What are you thinking about, my Darcy?" He put the tray of food on the dark wood coffee table and unloaded its bounty. Then seated himself on the teal couch and patted the cushion next to him. "You look sad."

My Darcy. Who would call her his Darcy in Seattle? The mailman?

"I'm thinking about my trip."

"What about it?" For once he didn't look uneasy when she brought it up. She didn't think she could stand the irony if he'd accepted her leaving before she had.

"It's not quite as…appealing as it used to be. I'll miss you. Horribly."

He smiled and touched her knee. "You don't have to go."

"I know."

He clinked their glasses again. "You don't have to decide tonight, either."

"Good." She drank some of the delicious champagne, relieved. For a second she thought he'd insist on her making a decision tonight. She should have known he wouldn't pressure her anymore. Even if she didn't decide until she was packed and ready to go with her key in the ignition.

"I used to want to travel when I was a boy." He leaned back, tossed a few cashews into his mouth.

"Where to?"

"Let's see. When we studied Greek mythology I wanted to go to Greece. When we studied Roman civilization I wanted to go to Italy. When I got interested in cooking I wanted to tour France, and when I watched *Star Trek*, I wanted to blast off into deep space."

"Did you ever get to those places?"

"Nope. Not one."

"Do you regret it?"

He raised an eyebrow over the rim of his glass. "I figure at thirty-two I have a few years before I can't even be rolled onto an airplane anymore."

Darcy giggled, feeling slightly foolish. And then as his eyes continued to examine her, she began to think he was making a rather unsubtle observation which she rather dimly didn't get at first.

Except that the point of her trip was to experience all the different cities alone. Because…

She drank more champagne. Something about turning into a different person. Except then she looked at Tyler and thought about who she was and how she felt around him, and she was no longer quite so sure she wanted to be anyone but who she was right now and to hell with her potential. Or was that the champagne and her hormones talking?

Nothing was clear, and after her third, fourth and fifth gulps of champagne, she didn't care. After her second glass, drinking interrupted occasionally by tucking into his delicious feast, not only was everything unclear, it was also fuzzy and tickly and quite funny.

Like when he told her about the time Cam bet him that he couldn't get Matti Davis to kiss him, and he'd stalked her determinedly one day, talking so hard and trying so desperately to charm her, that he didn't realize he'd followed her into the girls' bathroom until he heard the screams.

Then she told him about her smuggled-in hot outfit and how Evan Jacobus had been so deeply moved by her uncharacteristic show of skin, and how furious her father had been.

"So you've been a wild thing from the beginning, huh?"

"More of a wild-thing wannabe."

"Good thing Cam didn't know."

"Ha. He'd never look at me."

"I am quite sure he would." He put his champagne on the

table and pulled her close to him. "Probably steal you away from me."

"No chance." She put her glass next to his and wrapped her arms around his neck. "Nothing could."

"Not even a trip to Seattle, Los Angeles, Miami and Boston?" He lay back on the couch, dragging her with him.

"Not tonight." She pressed her lips to his, her hair spilling over on both sides, curtaining their kisses.

"How about never?" He slid the straps of her dress down over her shoulders, found the zipper in the middle of her back and slowly pulled it down.

"I'm thinking about it."

"Keep thinking." His hands were warm on her bare back, loosening the material further. She lifted up and let it fall partway down.

He sucked in his breath at the sight of her breasts, which she'd stuffed into a black lace demi-bra that made her look worthy of a *Playboy* spread.

Then those warm hands were on her breasts, gentle, barely touching, rubbing her nipples with flat palms until she felt them unfurling.

"I promised myself to wait until much, much later to get you out of your clothes, Darcy. What is it that you do to me?"

"Same thing you do to me," she whispered. "Turn me into a crazed nymphomaniac."

"Ah. No. You already were one. You just didn't know it."

"Until I met you?"

"And had the sudden desire to take off your clothes when I was at your window."

"Mmm, right, so I did."

He gave a wicked smile. "Take them off now."

"Yes, sir." But instead of obeying orders where she lay, she slid off the couch and strutted to the middle of the room, holding the bodice up. At center stage, she opened her arms and let the dress slide down, exposing her bra and matching black lace garter connected to black sheer stockings.

No panties.

Tyler moaned and had to reach into his pants for an immediate adjustment.

The familiar power surged. Darcy loved this woman she could become. How far could she go with her? "See anything you like?"

"All of it." He unzipped his fly, pulled down his briefs to release his erection, closed his fist over it. "Take the rest off."

"Yes, sir." She turned away from him, undulating her hips, then let her hands creep down her waist and back over her ass, stroking herself as she rotated her pelvis.

This time Tyler let out a growl that gave her more confidence, more power, and turned her on like mad. "Take. Everything. Off."

She raised her arms high, then bent forward, offering him the back view of her long legs, made longer by the torturous heels, her hair swinging free, the naked folds of her sex clearly visible to him. "When I'm ready."

Tyler gave another moan, this time in frustration. Darcy chuckled like a seasoned villainess, positive she'd never had this much fun or been this sure of herself. And the fun had only started. She reached one hand around and spread the lips of her sex for him, let him have a good look, then dipped one finger briefly inside her and painted the surrounding flesh with moisture. The same finger went into her mouth next, where she sucked as if it were that certain special part of him he loved having her lips around.

At that point, she thought he was going to have an apoplectic fit.

Instead, he hurriedly shed his pants and wrapped his fingers back around his erection, moving his hand steadily up and down, looking haggard. She was having the time of her life. The shoemaker Marquis de Sade had nothing on what she was doing to poor Tyler.

"Come here."

She shook her head, licked her finger lingeringly and this time painted around her sex with moisture from her mouth before pushing her finger inside herself again, in and out, closing her eyes, parting her lips, moaning softly, enjoying her own arousal for his benefit.

"Over here. Straddle me." He rolled on a condom, sounding desperate. "Now."

She straightened and tossed him a pouty arrogant look over her shoulder. "Not till I'm ready."

"You're ready now." He lunged off the couch and grabbed her hips before she could get away. She squealed in mock terror, trying not to giggle as he shoved her forward so her elbows landed on the seat of a soft upholstered chair and her rear was in the air firmly controlled by his hands.

Her urge to laugh died when she felt his cock slide roughly inside her. The force of it sent a wave of heat surging through her, more intense when he started thrusting hard, pushing to the hilt and withdrawing, again and again and again, rocking her body, swinging her breasts, bouncing her head off the cushioned back of the chair.

"Say you can't leave me." In. Out. In. Out.

"No. No." She panted the words. "I can't." She couldn't. Couldn't even think about it. Not with the way he was driving her to a total loss of control.

"Say it again." He withdrew nearly all the way, waited for her answer.

"I can't."

He drove in hard, pulled out. "Again."

"I can't!"

In hard. Out. "Again."

"Don't tease. Give it back to me."

He groaned and relented, resumed his rough, steady rhythm. "Yes, yes. Like that."

The combination pleasure-pain grew more intense, and she whimpered and reached between her legs to rub herself, desperate for release. Her body heated further; she cried out, then again, and he sped his pumping furiously until she slowly reached for the pinnacle and hung there for a beautiful suspended few seconds…before coming down the other side in a rush of contractions punctuated by gasps of pleasure.

He pushed in slowly, then thrust again, harder, gripped her hips and pulsed inside her, his breath driven harshly out of him by his own climax.

Apparently she liked it rough. Apparently so did he.

They stayed still, silent except for deep, ragged breathing, until Darcy lifted herself up from her elbows onto her hands and Tyler pulled out, gentle now, ran his hand up her back and helped her stand.

She staggered a little. "I think my muscles froze in that position."

"Hmm, really?" He held her while she worked the kinks out of her legs. "I can see a few bright sides to that."

"Ha." She turned and went into his arms, smiling, bold, confident, utterly alive and utterly female.

His answering smile warmed his blue-green eyes and crinkled them around the edges and she swore the room seemed to get brighter.

I love you. She wanted to say the words so badly it almost hurt. But how could she say them and then leave? Hell, how could she leave regardless of what she said?

He bent and kissed her then—long, slow, sweet kisses that touched every part of her heart and left her clinging to him afterward in a floaty and pathetically weakened state, even worse than after he'd made love to her so thoroughly and deliciously violently and so, so well.

"That was amazing, Tyler."

"No kidding. You are…" He shook his head, chuckling. "Let's just say I could do that again sometime."

"Me, too." She nodded bravely, feeling a bit sick since chances were slim that they could do it again before she left, which for some reason he didn't seem to mind tonight.

"How about dessert now?"

Darcy put a hand to her abdomen. "I don't think I have room."

"Of course you do."

They dressed again and he led her back to the couch, where she sat with him, closer this time, with her thigh pressed to his. But while she felt drained and, as usual, confused, not to mention sexually drugged, Tyler seemed to have been jazzed up by their lovemaking. She wasn't sure she'd ever seen him so energized, which seemed odd for their last night together. Maybe that was how he dealt with stress?

"When my sister Katie was little, she used to tell Mom she had a whole separate dessert stomach which was always empty, even when her other stomach was too full for broccoli."

Darcy's laughter came out rather wistfully, because while she enjoyed the story, she was also wishing she could be part of a family again. Maybe someday. Maybe she would want to come back home to Milwaukee after her travels. Eight years. Would he even still be here? Maybe she could come home sooner. Maybe she wouldn't go…

Tyler went into the kitchen and came back with scoops of homemade strawberry gelato and homemade chocolate biscotti, and Katie must have been right about the dessert stomach, because along with a tiny bit more champagne to help finish the bottle, both gelato and biscotti were going down quite nicely.

Until Darcy thought about what it would be like to be married to Tyler and able to eat this well all the time. She could learn a lot from him in the kitchen. She'd already learned tons in the bedroom.

"I can't eat another bite." She succumbed to melancholy and put down her mostly eaten biscotti.

"There's one more thing I have planned for tonight."

She held up her hands. "I can't. Really, I can't. I have no more stomachs."

"This one doesn't need a stomach."

She stared at him curiously. He was practically quivering with excitement. Had he invented some new zero-calorie chocolate spray? "Okay."

"All I need is your hand. Your left one."

She stuck out her left hand, and then it dawned on her what men in love sometimes needed left hands for and she started to feel scared and a little panicky. He couldn't be. He wouldn't. She wasn't ready, God, she wasn't *nearly* ready for that. She had too much to do, too many places to explore. She wasn't scheduled to settle down for eight more *years*.

"Darcy." He knelt and held her hand—her left one, help— and she wanted to stand up and scream, "Nooooooo!" and run out of the house, except there was always the chance she was wrong about his intentions. She desperately hoped so.

"You know I love you. You know I want you to stay here with me. I've never met anyone who fit me so well, who moves me so deeply, who brings out parts of me I didn't know I had, or at least parts of me I'd long ago lost touch with."

Oh, God. It was coming. She was sure now. What was she going to do?

"I know we haven't known each other long, but I am surer of what I want to do now than I've ever been of anything before in my life." He put his hand in his pocket and pulled out—she

knew what it was, but she refused to look. Instead she stared
steadily into his eyes, which were blurry and swimming because
tears were coming into hers, tears she was sure he'd mistake for
joy. Then the cool slide of metal on her fourth finger and his
husky voice again. "Darcy. My Darcy. Will you marry me?"

Half of her was dying to say yes...but only half. He must
know that. How could he do this to her?

His eyes got too intense, so she stared at her hand, which
was shaking, tears falling on it in hot splashy circles. Between
blinks her eyes cleared enough to see that the ring was one of
the most beautiful she'd ever seen—simple and elegant, but not
at all intimidating. It fit her finger the same way it fit her personality, as if it had been made for her. The same way he fit her.

But the world was pressing rewind on her again. Asking her
to change her life for a man, become tied to a city because of
a man, unable to explore her own identity apart from a man.
Those things really meant something to her, even in the face of
what might be True Love.

"Tyler. It's...beautiful."

He smiled in a tight strained way and she looked back into
his eyes and realized he was terrified. And then she remembered
Annie, and how Tyler realized she was slipping away and he'd
panicked and asked her to marry him to keep her with him, not
because they were right for each other. And she knew then that
she was going to break his heart by doing the right thing.

Even though sitting here now with this perfect ring on her
finger and the man she loved kneeling in front of her, hopeful
and scared, she knew it was the absolute last thing in the
universe she wanted to do.

16

DARCY LOOKED DUBIOUSLY around the apartment in a high-rise in Seattle's waterfront district. It was, without question, one of the most gorgeous places she'd ever been in. Hardwood floors, enormous kitchen with built-in stainless appliances, luxurious dining room, two huge bedrooms, floor-to-ceiling windows with views of Seattle on one side and the harbor on the other, an expansive curving outdoor terrace/balcony.

Luxury, location and…she couldn't think of another L-word except "lame."

"Isn't this fantastic?" The real estate agent, Denise, who appeared to be made of some kind of extraordinarily mobile plastic, turned rapturously then stopped in a model's pose, one foot pointed delicately in front of the other.

"Fantastic." There wasn't a thing wrong with the place. It was the perfect wild, wealthy single woman's dream-palace, exactly what Darcy had fantasized about when she'd imagined herself living the high life here.

Only she didn't want it. She hadn't wanted the last one, either. Or the one before that. However many there'd been— they'd all started to look the same.

Denise probably hated her.

Once again, she extracted herself from the real estate agent's clutches with a brochure and a promise to call the next day, and walked by herself down Stewart Street toward Western Avenue and the city's Waterfront Park. Seattle was wonderful. This area enchanted her. The art museum, the aquarium, Pike Place Market, everything. She'd been here a month, indulging in a whirlwind tour of the city and its environs, more and more enamored with what she found. A clean, manageable, extremely livable city, populated by friendly and helpful people. The climate was mild and pleasant—not as much rain as everyone elsewhere seemed to think. Everything about it was perfect.

Except how she felt in it.

Of course all she needed was time, she knew that. Who didn't? Time and a new home. She'd found a furnished apartment to rent by the week at only slightly less than the rates at the glorious Alexis hotel, where she'd stayed her first week, alternating between feeling like Paris Hilton and feeling like hell. Now the Midwesterner in her needed a place she could settle.

Except she couldn't settle on a place. She wanted a condo or an apartment that would feel like home, and nothing did. Maybe she was subconsciously looking for another Wauwatosa or Milwaukee, maybe some small stubborn part of her was still unwilling to let go of her town. Maybe she simply needed to go ahead, take the condo she just saw and trust that she'd grow to fit it. After all, she was here to explore different parts of herself, right? Maybe the luxury-condo side of her needed a nudge in the right direction.

If only it hadn't turned out to be so hard to leave Wisconsin. Molly and Bruce had thrown her a farewell party the night after she'd rejected Tyler's too-soon proposal—which had cemented her decision to come here, because what could you do after you broke the heart of the man you loved, as well as your own, but leave town?

Many more people had showed up than she'd expected. Everyone had a great time as only a crowd of good friends could, though Darcy would have had more fun if her heart were still intact. Molly and Bruce were such hospitable and loving people, even though they both wanted to strangle her for turning Tyler down. Even their kids had behaved.

Truly, Darcy had been overwhelmed by the loyalty of her buddies, touched by their sincere assertions that they'd miss her. Many of them she hadn't seen in a long time since she'd been so immersed in caring for her sick loved ones, and after so long it was like discovering new faces on old friends. Doubly hard to leave. The warmth in the room when Molly presented her gifts—a practical assortment of travel items and, from Bruce, a light-up rotating vibrator, thank him not at all—had enveloped her like a fifty-person hug.

Did she mention very hard to leave?

She arrived at Pike Place Market and was suddenly not in the mood for the jostling crowds of tourists and locals perusing the mind-boggling array of seafood, specialty items, gourmet food, produce and crafts for sale, so she turned left toward Second Avenue and her temporary home.

Temporary. Not home.

Inside she tossed her light sweater on someone else's chair, went into the kitchen and poured water into someone else's glass.

Maybe it was time she made some new friends besides the guy at the paper kiosk and the woman at the nearby bakery. Since finding a home had been her first priority, Darcy had put off exploring classes and volunteer options, which would be the easiest way to get to know people. Finding them now would take extra effort.

Okay, then. She'd make that effort. Today was officially the end of mourning her old life and love. Tonight she'd dress up, visit a bar, make friends, maybe meet a man, and really start her new life.

Done.

After a mediocre dinner made in someone else's kitchen, eaten off someone else's plates, she watched someone else's TV for a while until she decided it was late enough for Seattle night-life to have gotten started.

Alors…

She'd brought Angel's wild, black leather outfit, which would be perfect for her introduction to Pacific Northwestern club-hopping society. Except this time when she put it on, instead of feeling über-sexy and excited and full of fun, she felt half-naked and slutty.

Blech. Ptooey.

So far every day had been a long, drawn-out version of the disorienting disconnect she'd experienced when she first stepped into Starlight City dressed as Angel. Too many things about this trip so far had fallen flat, as if they were yet more fantasies gone wrong.

But look how well the night at Starlight had turned out after she rode the feeling for a while and mastered it. Right? Right. Except it had been Tyler who—

She pulled down the silver zippers in exasperation and tossed the leather across the spacious bedroom that wasn't hers.

Okay, Darcy, major attitude adjustment needed. She didn't want to be Angel tonight? Fine. Good. No problem. She'd put on jeans and a plain top and just go. If she spent another night tagging along with tourist crowds or home watching TV, they'd have to lock her away somewhere with nice soft walls. She'd come here to live it up, and live it up she was going to.

Or else.

Except…it really bothered her that she'd come all this way to go out in jeans and a boring red top. She could be doing that in Milwaukee, where she'd have plenty of people to go with. Like Tyler. And Tyler. And hey, how about…Tyler?

Help.

She put up her hands to tell the tears, "Keep back." Stop. Now. Hold everything. Had she not *just* said that her attitude needed adjusting?

She was in a wonderful city. She'd make new friends. She never had trouble making friends.

Her phone rang and she jumped at the unaccustomed sound. "Hello?"

"It's Mo-o-lly!"

"Molly, hi!" A wave of homesickness washed over her as it did every time Molly called, which wasn't as often as Darcy wanted, but Molly had her hands full and Darcy's loneliness wasn't her problem. This was Darcy's new life and she had charged herself with making it work for herself, by herself.

Right. Okay. Got that straight.

"How's things in the Dairy State?" She kept her tone cheerful as she always did, since she was sure Molly kept Tyler apprised of everything that was happening to her, and doubly sure they were both waiting eagerly for her to fall on her face. Despite a rough start, she was not ready to do that yet.

"Very fertile."

Darcy laughed. "Them cows growing like weeds?"

"No. Ver-r-r-ry fertile."

"Omigod!" Darcy gasped. "You're pregnant already?"

"Yup. Just found out last night, and of course besides Bruce and our families, you're the first to know."

"Oh, wow. Oh, Molly." Darcy's eyes filled with tears. "That is so incredible."

"Uh-huh. Knock wood, but I never miscarried before, so if all goes well this time, too, the little bug is due March twenty-second."

"March, oh, wow. I can't wait to—" She stopped, sick at heart. She wouldn't be there. If she wanted to see Molly's baby, she'd have to fly home, then fly back. She wouldn't get to know the child until it was nearly eight years old, and if she decided not to move back to Milwaukee, then she'd never have a close relationship with Molly's third child at all. That seemed impossible.

"Maybe you can fly out after the birth for a visit."

"Sure. Sure. Of course I will." Of course she would. A weekend. Two days. A six-hour, two-flight trip each way. Minimum.

"So? Everything is going well?"

"Really well, yeah." She hated lying and didn't know why she bothered because Molly could always tell. "I looked at more condos today and I think I've found one I really like. Oh, and I'm looking for a place to take evening classes. Maybe I can eventually teach some. And there are all kinds of wonderful—"

"You're miserable, aren't you?"

"Molly." She laughed, unconvincingly. "No, I'm not. I mean, it's an adjustment and everything, but—"

"Bruce is taking Tyler out for a drink on Friday at Hector's. I don't think he's done anything but paint and mope since you've been gone."

"Oh." The syllable was tiny and sad and guilty. "I...well, tell him I said...hi."

Hi. How painfully inadequate was that?

"Okay. I gotta give Kyle his bath. You have fun pretending to enjoy yourself."

"Molly..."

"You belong here, Darcy. With Tyler. But I, of course, will not interfere at all."

"Of course not." A tear rolled down her cheek. Would she ever get over this pain?

"I just want you to be happy."

She bit her lip, forced her voice to come out normally. "I know. Thanks, Moll. I'm *so* thrilled for you. Give Bruce a hug."

"Will do!"

Darcy hung up and sank into the ugly blue chair that she'd never have bought in a million years.

Well. She had two choices. She could sit here and cry and feel sorry for herself and question everything she'd spent so long deciding was the right path for her to take.

Or she could go out.

Half an hour later, she was inside the Baltic Room, which an Internet search had turned up as an appealing prospect, perusing the casual jeans-clad crowd, thanking God she hadn't turned up in mini leather. She would have felt like a freak.

Except no one at Starlight City had been wearing leather except her, and she'd done fine after that first odd disoriented moment. All she'd had to do to feel right was to think of Tyler and how easy and exciting it had been to seduce him.

Oh, no. She couldn't think about that now. Bawling in the middle of a bar wouldn't get her the kind of attention she wanted. She'd come here for fun and friends, and damn it, she was going to find both.

The place was crowded but not packed, with plenty of good-looking wholesome guys and nice-looking women. The ambience was classy, cherry walls and bar, high ceiling covered with twinkling fiber-optic stars. Lucite tables glowed under their lamps; lots of people were dancing and the music was good.

She squeezed up to the bar, ordered a drink, downed it, ordered another and turned determinedly to introduce herself to Seattle's young hot singles. *Okay, Darcy. See what's happening here.* Several guys in a nearby group were checking her out. She glanced carefully, trying to figure out which one to smile at and encourage. Not that one. Not that one. Maybe—

Her stomach bottomed out. The back of some guy's head

looked almost exactly like Tyler's. For a crazy second she thought Molly had somehow gotten him here tonight, but then, of course, no one knew she was here.

No one. In the entire vastness of the universe.

This was the pits.

She didn't want to be here. She wanted to be back in Milwaukee where everyone knew her and she knew everyone. Where she could wear black leather and think about Tyler and feel better. And see Tyler and feel more than better. And with Tyler be the woman she'd always...

Oh, my God. Darcy, you idiot. It was him. It was *Tyler.*

He hadn't kept her from exploring different sides of herself. He'd allowed her to. With him she felt completely safe being whoever she wanted to be. Here...well, just look at her. Tonight was the first night in a month she'd felt like going out. She'd had to drag herself to go, and she'd worn boring clothes and was completely interchangeable with any other female in the room.

But not to Tyler. Never to Tyler. Even in a T-shirt and boxers with morning breath, messy hair and no makeup, she was the woman she'd always wanted to be to him. And with him.

One of the guys broke off from the group and approached her. Very good-looking, college-boy aura, not threatening, not sleazy...not Tyler.

"Hi there. You enjoying the music?"

She nodded. "Hey, have you seen a tall, blue-green-eyed, dark-haired guy, probably wearing a blue shirt and jeans, most likely with little paint flecks in his hair? He's my fiancé, and he's not here."

His face fell. "Fiancé, huh? Haven't seen him, no. But if I do, I'll tell him you're looking for him."

"Actually—" she downed her second drink and gave him a brilliant smile "—I think I'll go after him myself."

"SORRY, WHAT DID YOU SAY?" Tyler jerked his attention from the vision of Darcy inside his head to Bruce, sitting with him at the bar at Hector's.

Bruce rolled his eyes. "Tyler, my man, I would bet you haven't heard a thing I've said to you all night."

"Sorry. Sorry." Tyler pushed his beer away. "I guess I'm distracted."

"You've been distracted for the past month. This is the first time I've been able to get you to go out."

"I know."

"Your life has to go on at some point."

"I know, Bruce."

"You can't mope over this woman for the entire—"

"*Right*. Right. I get it." He dragged his hands down over his face. "Sorry."

"Besides—" Bruce flicked a glance to the huge TV showing the Brewers game behind the bar "—Molly is sure she'll come back."

Tyler lifted a cynical eyebrow. "Well, if Molly says…"

"Hey, I'm telling you." Bruce spread his hands out. "The woman knows what she's talking about."

"I don't think she's right this time." He hooked his finger through the handle of his beer mug. "It was my fault Darcy left. The last thing you do to a woman who is fed up with being tied down is try to tie her down."

"Hey, you went with what you were feeling. There's nothing wrong with that. Love has to be honest." He thumped a fist over his heart. "It's not about strategy."

"Yeah. I guess."

A collective shout went up in the bar. Bruce threw up his hands. "Home run! Brewers lead it five to three!"

Tyler clapped a few times, barely glancing at the screen. Yeah. Go Brewers.

"Listen, I've been meaning to tell you. This personal trainer I've been telling you about, Lolita. She just got dumped by her boyfriend and I was thinking maybe you and she…"

"The one that looks like—"

"Yep. And she's a sweetheart. Real class act. A body that will keep you up a-a-all night. Not that such a thing is important to sensitive men of substance like us, of course."

Tyler forced himself to chuckle. "Of course."

"What do you say?"

"I don't think so."

"She's not looking for anything serious. On the rebound, both of you." He punched Tyler's shoulder. "Just go out and have fun, for God's sake. You're starting to depress *me*."

Tyler gazed into the depth of his beer, where a disturbing black speck lurked in the bottom of the glass. He should jump at the chance. What harm could it do? But obviously he hadn't remotely let go of Darcy, because even considering going out with another woman made him uneasy and guilty.

Which was crazy. Who knew what *she* was doing? Dressed in tight leather, picking up Seattle's hottest men one after another, having sex with them all over the city…

Pain seared. It never did seem to get easier.

"It's too soon for me, Bruce."

Bruce threw up his hands. "I give up. I'll call Molly and get Darcy's address. She talked to her a few days ago and knows where she's staying. You get on the Internet and book a stinking plane to Seattle. You belong with her? Go get her."

"You think I haven't thought of that?" Tyler's strangled shout made the guy behind Bruce actually take his eyes off the TV screen. "That's exactly what I *shouldn't* do. If I had half a brain I would have realized that. If I hadn't tried to force her into staying by marrying me, she might have stayed here on her own. I made the same mistake with Annie. I have to let her come to me."

"I see." Bruce nodded slowly, face unusually serious, voice oddly singsongy. "If you love someone, set her free. If she doesn't come back, she was never meant to be yours..."

Tyler laughed honestly for the first time in well over a week. "You ever thought of writing that down? Might make a good T-shirt."

"Ya think?" Bruce grinned widely and slapped him on the back. "You're probably right about not going after her. I hope she comes back. And not just because you're driving me crazy."

"Thanks, Bruce. So do I." He finished as much of his beer as he could without disturbing the ominous black speck. "I'm done in. Spent the day prepping another house. Think I'll go. Thanks for the beer and the advice."

"Sure." Bruce raised his hand and Tyler slapped it. "Take care, my man."

"You, too." He left the crowded noisy bar and stepped into the cool night air with relief. Waiting for Darcy to come to her senses—at least that's how he saw it—was the hardest thing he'd ever done. Because her epiphany could happen now or any time over the next eight years. Or it could never happen at all. How long was reasonable to hope? At what point could he say, okay, this is it, she's not coming back, I need to move on?

No answers. No one to ask. Darcy still probably didn't even know.

He walked to his car, drove home with the same sick weight in his chest that had been there since Darcy had rejected his ring and his heart. Katie had been right about love at first sight, but wrong about taking that kind of risk with Darcy. Cam had been the gambler. Tyler should have kept on playing it safe, which fit him better.

His home on 64th Street looked dark and unwelcoming; he'd forgotten to turn on the outdoor lights.

Car parked in the garage, button punched to lower the door, he walked down the driveway to the side door and let himself in. He was dead tired, but he knew he wouldn't sleep. Again. Maybe he'd numb his brain with some TV. Funny, he probably now felt about his life here the way Darcy used to feel. But for Tyler, it wasn't about Milwaukee or Wauwatosa, it was about Darcy.

In his living room, he didn't bother turning on a light, just opened the doors to his entertainment center and sank onto the couch, pointed the remote dispiritedly at the set. Then dropped his hand, not even in the mood to watch.

Nothing was good without Darcy.

A movement caught his eye by the French window at the southwest corner of his house. He turned, but only saw Annika's slow lumbering walk down the block on the other side of the street, lit brightly as she passed under a streetlight, with Scotty the Scottie undoubtedly trotting behind her.

He pointed the remote at the set again. Great. Another excitement to add to his exciting evening repertoire: sitting in the dark seeing things that weren't there.

Another movement. He dropped his hand and looked again. Annika was still there, standing while Scotty probably did his business, but it was hard to see her because something was in the way, something close by. Right outside his window. Something that looked like a…

Breast.

He must be losing it. He blinked. Blinked again. Stood and took a step toward the window.

Then froze.

Darcy.

Okay, now he was hallucinating. Darcy was in Seattle. All

he could really see was the dark shape of a woman outside his window.

A woman taking off her clothes.

His cock responded immediately. His conscious brain took slightly longer to catch up to the fact that his instinct and penis were correct.

Darcy Wolf was standing outside his window. Stripping.

He started to grin, and once he started, the grin got wider and wider and he was pretty sure he'd be grinning like a complete fool for the rest of his life. He flipped on a light and the silhouette came to life in flesh tones he didn't think he'd see for a long, long time, if ever again.

She was—

"Darcy Wolf, is that you?"

He was at the window in two steps, opened it, yanked the levers to release the screen and pushed it out so she'd have a space wide enough to climb through.

"Oh, my God, it's Annika!" Darcy tried and failed to cover her most beautiful parts. Not enough hands, too much skin. Fine by him. "I didn't see her."

"Here." He was laughing so hard he could barely speak. "Take my hand. Here."

"Young lady, are you naked?"

"What's going on out there?" Another voice, male, shouting across the street. *"Is there a problem?"*

"Oh, *no!*" Darcy's whisper shot up into a squeal of horror. She grabbed her clothes and then his hand.

He pulled hard; she found footing on the stone and climbed through. Tyler immediately latched the screen, closed and locked the window. "C'mon. Upstairs."

In his bedroom, safely away from any prying eyes from the street, he closed his arms around her so hard she coughed for lack of air. "You're here."

"I'm here. I'm so sorry it took me so long to figure out where I belong."

"Where is that?" He wanted to hear her say it.

She hugged him back hard enough to make his ribs creak. "Here. With you. Wearing your ring, if you still have it."

Then nothing was said for a long, long time, because he planned to kiss her for a solid hour to make up for all the kissing he hadn't been able to do in the last month. The room was dark, a breeze flowed through his open windows with the promise of summer. Her lips were warm, eager, her taste so erotically familiar that he—

"You're saying there was a *naked woman?* Out *here?*" The man was clearly skeptical.

"Yes," Annika's voice answered. "Right here. That Darcy Wolf. She's in Seattle now."

Tyler had his hand over his mouth to keep from laughing. Darcy's face was pressed against his chest; her body shook.

"Come on, Annika," the man said wearily. "I'll walk you home."

"Oh, dear." Annika's voice wavered a little. "I was so sure I— Well, okay. Thank you, Bob. Home sounds good. Really, really good."

Their footsteps clumped on the driveway, swished over his lawn, then clumped again on the sidewalk and faded up 64th Street.

"Tyler?"

"Mmm?" He stroked her hair, sure he'd never want to stop touching her, just to make sure she was really real and really here.

"For once I agree with Annika." Even in the near darkness he could see her beautiful face smiling up at him, and his heart swelled with so much love he could barely take in what was happening. She was back. She'd marry him. They could spend the rest of their lives having sex all over the city of Milwaukee. And they'd start by doing it tonight, right here, right now.

"What did Annika say that you could possibly agree with?"

She laughed, that beautiful laugh he loved so much, and started walking him backward toward the bed and the rest of their lives together. "She said, 'Home sounds good.'"

He grinned and fell with her, in love from his very first sight all the way until his last. "Really, really good."

* * * * *

THOROUGHBRED LEGACY
The stakes are high when it comes to love,
horse racing, family secrets
and broken promises.

A new exciting Harlequin continuity series coming soon!
Led by New York Times *bestselling author Elizabeth Bevarly*
FLIRTING WITH TROUBLE

Here's a preview!

THE DOOR CLOSED behind them, throwing them into darkness and leaving them utterly alone. And the next thing Daniel knew, he heard himself saying, "Marnie, I'm sorry about the way things turned out in Del Mar."

She said nothing at first, only strode across the room and stared out the window beside him. Although he couldn't see her well in the darkness—he still hadn't switched on a light...but then, neither had she—he imagined her expression was a little preoccupied, a little anxious, a little confused.

Finally, very softly, she said, "Are you?"

He nodded, then, worried she wouldn't be able to see the gesture, added, "Yeah. I am. I should have said goodbye to you."

"Yes, you should have."

Actually, he thought, there were a lot of things he should have done in Del Mar. He'd had *a lot* riding on the Pacific Classic, and even more on his entry, Little Joe, but after meeting Marnie, the Pacific Classic had been the last thing on Daniel's mind. His loss at Del Mar had pretty much ended his career before it had even begun, and he'd had to start all over again, rebuilding from nothing.

He simply had not then and did not now have room in his life for a woman as potent as Marnie Roberts. He was a horseman first and foremost. From the time he was a schoolboy, he'd known what he wanted to do with his life—be the best possible trainer he could be.

He had to make sure Marnie understood—and he understood, too—why things had ended the way they had eight years ago. He just wished he could find the words to do that. Hell, he wished he could find the *thoughts* to do that.

"You made me forget things, Marnie, things that I really needed to remember. And that scared the hell out of me. Little Joe should have won the Classic. He was by far the best horse entered in that race. But I didn't give him the attention he needed and deserved that week, because all I could think about was you. Hell, when I woke up that morning all I wanted to do was lie there and look at you, and then wake you up and make love to you again. If I hadn't left when I did—the way I did— I might still be lying there in that bed with you, thinking about nothing else."

"And would that be so terrible?" she asked.

"Of course not," he told her. "But that wasn't why I was in Del Mar," he repeated. "I was in Del Mar to win a race. That was my job. And my work was the most important thing to me."

She said nothing for a moment, only studied his face in the darkness as if looking for the answer to a very important question. Finally she asked, "And what's the most important thing to you now, Daniel?"

Wasn't the answer to that obvious? "My work," he answered automatically.

She nodded slowly. "Of course," she said softly. "That is, after all, what you do best."

Her comment, too, puzzled him. She made it sound as if being good at what he did was a bad thing.

She bit her lip thoughtfully, her eyes fixed on his, glimmering in the scant moonlight that was filtering through the window. And damned if Daniel didn't find himself wanting to pull her into his arms and kiss her. But as much as it might have felt as if no time had passed since Del Mar, there were eight years between now and then. And eight years was a long time in the best of circumstances. For Daniel and Marnie, it was virtually a lifetime.

So Daniel turned and started for the door, then halted. He couldn't just walk away and leave things as they were, unsettled. He'd done that eight years ago and regretted it.

"It *was* good to see you again, Marnie," he said softly. And since he was being honest, he added, "I hope we see each other again."

She didn't say anything in response, only stood silhouetted against the window with her arms wrapped around her in a way that made him wonder whether she was doing it because she was cold, or if she just needed something—someone—to hold on to. In either case, Daniel understood. There was an emptiness clinging to him that he suspected would be there for a long time.

* * * * *

THOROUGHBRED LEGACY
Coming soon wherever books are sold!

Thoroughbred *Legacy*

Launching in June 2008

A dramatic new 12-book continuity that embodies the American Dream.

Meet the Prestons, owners of Quest Stables, a successful
horse-racing and breeding empire. But the lives, loves
and reputations of this hardworking family are put at risk
when a breeding scandal unfolds.

Flirting with Trouble

by *New York Times* bestselling author

ELIZABETH BEVARLY

Eight years ago, publicist Marnie Roberts spent seven days
of bliss with Australian horse trainer Daniel Whittleson.
But just as quickly, he disappeared. Now Marnie is
heading to Australia to finally confront the man
she's never been able to forget.

*The stakes are high when it comes to love, horse racing,
family secrets and broken promises.*

A new exciting Harlequin continuity series coming soon!

REQUEST YOUR FREE BOOKS!

2 FREE NOVELS PLUS 2 FREE GIFTS!

HARLEQUIN®

Blaze™

Red-hot reads!

HB08

Cole's Red-Hot Pursuit

Cole Westmoreland is a man who gets what he
wants. And he wants independent and sultry
Patrina Forman! She resists him—until a Montana
blizzard traps them together. For three delicious
nights, Cole indulges Patrina with his brand of
seduction. When the sun comes out, Cole and
Patrina are left to wonder—will this be the end of
the passion that storms between them?

Look for

COLE'S RED-HOT
PURSUIT

by USA TODAY bestselling author

BRENDA
JACKSON

Available in June 2008 wherever you buy books.

Always Powerful, Passionate and Provocative.

HARLEQUIN®

Blaze™

COMING NEXT MONTH

#399 CROSSING THE LINE Lori Wilde
Perfect Anatomy
Confidential Rejuvenations, an exclusive Texas boutique clinic, has a villain on
the loose. But it's the new surgeon, Dr. Dante Nash, who is getting the most
attention from chief nurse Elle Kingston....

#400 THE LONER Rhonda Nelson
Men Out of Uniform
Lucas "Huck" Finn is thrilled to join Ranger Security—until he learns his new
job is to babysit Sapphira Stravos, a doggie-toting debutante. Still, he knows
there's more to Sapphira than meets the eye. And what's meeting the eye is
damn hard to resist.

#401 NOBODY DOES IT BETTER Jennifer LaBrecque
Lust in Translation
Gage Carswell, British spy, is all about getting his man—or in this case, his
woman. He's after Holly Smith, whom he believes to be a notorious agent. And
he's willing to do anything—squire her around Venice, play out all her sexual
fantasies—to achieve his goal. Too bad this time *his* woman isn't the *right* woman.

#402 SLOW HANDS Leslie Kelly
The Wrong Bed: Again and Again
Heiress Madeleine Turner only wants to stop her stepmother from making
a huge mistake. That's how she ends up buying Jake Wallace at a charity
bachelor auction. But now that she's won the sexy guy, what's she going to do
with him? Lucky for her, Jake has a few ideas....

#403 SEX BY THE NUMBERS Marie Donovan
Blush
Accountant—undercover! Pretending to be seriously sexy Dane Weiss's ditsy
personal assistant to secretly hunt for missing company funds isn't what
Keeley Davis signed up for. But the overtime is out of this world!

#404 BELOW THE BELT Sarah Mayberry
Jamie Sawyer wants to redeem her family name in the boxing world. To do that,
she needs trainer Cooper Fitzgerald. Spending time together ignites a sizzling
attraction...one he's resisting. Looks as if she'll have to aim her best shots a
little low to get what she wants.

www.eHarlequin.com

HBCNM0508